"I haven't found all the freckles yet . . ."

Ted's husky voice sent shivers up Kyla's spine. "I can't stop now," he murmured teasingly, kissing her shoulder.

"Please, don't," Kyla moaned as his warm lips traced wild patterns on her sensitive skin. Even in the aftermath of love, her body cried out for more.

"One hundred and twelve," he whispered in her ear. "Freckles," he added with a grin, in answer to her questioning look.

Kyla laughed, thinking how much she loved this man; there couldn't be anyone else for her.

"I'll never have enough of you," he said, his eyes hazy with desire.

"I hope not," she whispered, running a hand through his tousled hair.

"Do you want to be my wife, Kyla?" Ted's voice was serious now—quite different from a moment ago. "Do you want to be the mother of my children?"

Suddenly the world spun around Kyla. *Children.* The only thing she couldn't give him. How could she have fallen in love with a man who wanted more from life than she could offer?

Susan Gayle called on her years of experience as an R.N. while writing her first romance. *Temperature's Rising* is about a love affair that develops in the bustle of a hospital emergency room—Susan's home ground. The novel reached the finals of the Romance Writers of America Golden Heart Contest, and needless to say, Susan was thrilled!

Married with two daughters, this up-and-coming author makes her home in Kansas City. She enjoys traveling and recently visited Denmark—the land of her forefathers. Susan is already busy working on her next novel.

Temperature's Rising

SUSAN GAYLE

Harlequin Books

TORONTO • NEW YORK • LONDON
AMSTERDAM • PARIS • SYDNEY • HAMBURG
STOCKHOLM • ATHENS • TOKYO • MILAN

In loving memory of my father,
my first real life hero

With special thanks to my daughter, Diane,
whose idea sparked this book

Published July 1990

ISBN 0-373-25407-5

1

THE AUTOMATIC double glass doors of Emergency slid open. Conditioned to the sound, Kyla Bradford glanced toward them, her senses on full alert despite the fact that Wallace Osgood, the hospital administrator, droned on relentlessly in her left ear. She'd been locked in conversation with him for the past twenty minutes. Now perhaps she could escape his latest tiresome explanation of hospital policy and get on with what she did best: tending to emergencies.

The emergency in question wavered on the threshold, his athletically lean body angled precariously against Jane, the tiny gray-haired admitting clerk.

Instinctively Kyla began her clinical assessment of him. His color was good. He had a healthy tan as if he spent a great deal of time outdoors. There were no beads of sweat dotting his forehead, just one curl, walnut brown and unruly, tumbling across it. His totally male frame fit snugly in a pair of well-worn jeans, she noted, her assesment losing its clinical practicality.

He appeared too superb a specimen to be seriously ill. Yet, from the way he clutched his side and bent double at the waist, it was obvious he was in distress.

She started toward him, but before she could take a full step in his direction, the administrator stopped her. "Miss Bradford, I'm not through speaking to you. You're the nursing supervisor of this department, not its one-woman staff. There are others on this unit capable of handling a simple emergency."

Before he'd even finished his statement, Leah, one of the evening nurses, appeared on the scene to relieve Jane of her intriguing burden and lead him into Treatment Room One. At times like this, Kyla wished she was not surrounded by such an efficient team.

"Yes, Wallace, you were saying . . ." With a sigh, she forced her attention back to the head of Woodland Memorial Hospital.

As Wallace continued his dry discourse about inconsequential hospital details, Kyla allowed her gaze to drift toward the first treatment room. Dr. Roger Mason, tonight's attending physician, had entered the room, followed soon after by a white-coated lab technician with his array of needles and collecting tubes. Dr. Mason, she knew, would have ordered blood tests, expecting a hot appendix.

Would the patient need surgery? she wondered, brushing at a straying tendril of her copper-colored hair, pushing it back into its French braid. Her mind had wandered again from Wallace's speech and was fixed on the scenario in the treatment room opposite her. With its miniblinds tilted at just the right angle, she could make out some movement but little else.

"Ahem, Miss Bradford," Wallace interjected. "I'm trying to discuss a matter of importance with you. Could you manage to tear your eyes away from what's going on in there and listen to me?"

Kyla's patience skated dangerously near the breaking point. One white duty shoe tapped a restless message against the tiled floor of the nursing station but she forced herself to remain silent. It wouldn't do to rile Wallace. Better to hear him out, she decided. Sooner or later he'd get to the real purpose of his unscheduled visit to the Emergency Room.

To her relief that moment came with his next breath.

"One final word of warning regarding the heart transplant surgery scheduled for tonight," he began, his voice taking on an even greater air of importance. "As you know, everything's set to begin as soon as the donor heart arrives. It will come through your department, sometime during your shift. So I want you to be on your toes—"

"I'll alert surgery the second the chartered helicopter touches down and escort the transport team to the Operating Room," Kyla interrupted, hoping to bring the conversation to an end. "Is there anything else?"

Wallace had issued bulletins all week about the possibility of the surgery and Emergency's role in it. This was Woodland Memorial's first heart transplant, and she knew he was uneasy about it. Still, there was a limit to tolerating his directives.

"Only this," he answered, scowling at her over the tops of his round wire eyeglasses. "I want no information given out to reporters. Leonard Daniels is entitled to his privacy in this hospital no matter how newsworthy his surgery might be. So be careful about what you say and to whom you say it. Do I make myself absolutely clear?"

Kyla nodded. "Don't you worry, Wallace. I can handle the press."

Reporters were an unfortunate fact of life around a busy inner-city hospital, and Kyla had had to chase off her share of the hungry newshounds who hung around the ER hoping for a story, any story, on a slow news night. Wallace had issued a statement to the press that afternoon and she hoped that would satisfy them, but she had her doubts.

Taking Wallace by the arm, she skillfully maneuvered him toward the door. "I have everything under control," she reassured him. When the electric eye was triggered, the glass panels slid open. He cast one last worried glance at her, but she tossed him a confident smile and sent him on his way.

"Whatever happened to administrators who spent all their time in their office or the boardroom?" She rolled her eyes at Jane seated behind the admitting desk.

Jane laughed and shoved a clipboard at her. "Just initial these and don't try to figure it out."

Kyla muttered something about what she'd like to do with all paperwork as she signed the pages and handed them back to her.

Returning to the nursing station she saw that Roger was still in the treatment room with the intriguing male patient who'd distracted her earlier. *What was it about him?* she puzzled, tapping the end of her pen against her lower lip. And when had she begun letting tall, handsome patients become a distraction anyway?

5:35 p.m., she noted, glancing at the large round clock on the wall. She hoped the heart would arrive soon. The reporters were beginning to gather like starving crows. She'd noticed them amassing outside Wallace's office when she'd come on duty this afternoon. Leonard Daniels, the heart transplant patient waiting in surgery, was an important man in the Kansas City business community, and the press wanted the story, she knew.

The Emergency Room was eerily quiet tonight. A feeling of restlessness washed over her as she looked around its starch-and-steel efficiency. Only three patients so far, including the one who'd thoroughly captivated her.

Captivated?

No, she decided. He'd merely piqued her curiosity.

Just then, Roger stepped out of the examining room, interrupting her thoughts. He was tall and rangy, pleasantly good-looking and single. Kyla liked him. They met for supper in the cafeteria when their hectic schedules permitted. Occasionally, he escorted her to hospital social functions, but there was never more between them than a comfortable friendship, an arrangement that suited them both.

The Emergency Room kept Kyla too busy to have time for serious dating. Most men she'd gone out with soon tired of waiting around for one of her free evenings.

Roger tunneled his fingers through his sandy hair and sauntered toward her, chart in hand. His usual wide boyish grin turned into a definite frown, Kyla noted. Her wide-set gray eyes scanned his face for the reason.

"What is it, Roger?" She sensed trouble.

He scrawled one last notation on the chart, then tossed it in front of her. "We've got ourselves a ringer in there." He aimed a finger in the direction of the treatment room.

"A reporter?"

"I'd bet money on it." He slumped into a chair beside her. "He claims to have right lower quadrant pain but he has no rebound tenderness, his white count is normal, no fever. Just an inordinate amount of curiosity about our transplant patient."

Kyla jumped up, nearly knocking over her chair. "This time those guys have gone too far," she exploded. Wallace had been concerned about meddling reporters, but she hadn't thought one of them would be so bold as to actually infiltrate the ER—the Emergency Room was her domain.

Just then Leah and the rest of the evening crew joined them at the nursing station. "What's up?" Leah asked.

"A reporter in Room One, posing as a patient," Kyla answered, her voice carrying the sharp edge of her anger.

"I'll call Security." Leah picked up the phone, but Kyla stopped her.

"No, wait. I'm going to get this guy and get him good." She brought one clenched fist down on the imposter's chart in front of her. This was her department and she was not about to tolerate any reporter's underhanded tactics.

Roger shot her a cautionary look. "Kyla, I don't know what you're up to, but whatever it is, forget it."

Kyla ignored his warning. Roger should already know he couldn't stop her once her mind was made up. This newsmonger needed to be taught a lesson, and she was just the person to do it. But how? Her mind searched for the perfect way to send him scuttling out of the unit with his tail tucked neatly between his legs.

When she spotted the housekeeping aide sloshing her unwieldy mop along the ER corridor, she knew just how she was going to do it.

"Mrs. Grady," she said, approaching the short plump woman, "you look like you could use a break." She eased the housekeeper toward the nursing lounge, leaving her friends wearing puzzled expressions. "Sit down. Put up your feet. Here." She led her toward the break room's worn-out sofa.

"I guess I don't mind if I do," Mrs. Grady replied, arranging her well-padded rump on the battered seat cushion.

Kyla smiled. "I need to borrow your smock and cleaning cart. There's a little something I need to—um—clean up."

The woman looked confused by Kyla's unusual request, but slipped out of her smock and handed it over before settling back into her cushy spot.

"What are you doing?" Leah asked as Kyla pulled on the garment.

Kyla didn't answer. She removed her stethoscope from around her neck and checked to see that her name tag and nursing pin were well concealed by the striped cover-up.

"Come on, Kyla. What gives? If you're going to do this, at least let us in on it," Roger demanded.

Kyla turned to him. "That newspaper article you were reading here last night about the zoo director—what was his name?"

"I don't know. Montana, I think. Yeah, Jack Montana. But—"

"Roger, in exactly five minutes I want you to have Jack Montana paged."

"Paged? Kyla—?"

"Just do it, Roger." She shot him a determined look, then shoved the cleaning cart through the door into Treatment Room One.

With her back to the patient on the gurney, she pulled on an oversized pair of yellow rubber gloves and poured cleaning solution into a small bucket. Finding a sponge on the cart, she soaked it in the disinfectant and began cleaning, waiting for the reporter to barrage her with questions. She was certain she wouldn't have to wait long.

At first there was only the sound of her sponge squeaking a soapy path across the chrome countertop. The silence nearly threw her off. Could Roger have been wrong about him? Was he really not a reporter but only a guy with belly pain who asked a lot of questions? No, he'd looked too good, too vital, to be sick. And then there were the objective findings—no fever, normal white count. This guy was a faker. She was sure of it.

"Don't you think that counter is clean by now?" When his voice finally came it surprised her. It was deep-timbred and as smooth as brass as it wafted across the small cubicle, curling around her senses, making her curiously aware of its masculine owner in a way she had not expected.

Managing a quick recovery, Kyla continued with the charade. "It has to be done daily," she responded, hoping her voice didn't quiver and give her away. She dipped the sponge into the solution, then wrung it out, waiting patiently for the right moment to drop her bombshell. "A hospital has to be clean."

"Ah, but of course. Especially one having a heart transplant."

Here it comes! Remain calm, don't look up, she cautioned herself. Her hand trembled slightly, but a smile twitched at the corners of her mouth.

"A surgery like that will give this hospital instant celebrity status. And the patient is an important man, not to mention, rich." He chuckled quietly behind her. "I suppose if he makes it, he'll want a Leonard A. Daniels Cardiac Wing built or something equally appropriate. That can't hurt Woodland Memorial."

His tone was casual, but Kyla knew just where the conversation was leading.

"I suppose," she replied, trying to keep her voice equally casual. "But it doesn't really concern me. I just clean up around this place." As if to prove that point, she moved the large glass jars containing cotton balls, tongue depressors and cotton-tipped applicators, running her sponge behind them, then setting them back in place.

"But you couldn't have missed all the talk. This place is really abuzz." Kyla heard the gurney frame clank as he shifted his weight on it. "I hear the donor heart is supposed to arrive any time now. It's coming in by helicopter."

Her hand stopped in mid-swipe and she raised her head. This guy had done his homework. She was certain Wallace hadn't given out this kind of information in his brief press conference. Wallace was a master of double-talk. She swung around to confront her interrogator.

At the sight of him, her heart slammed into *race*. Wearing only a sheet that read Property of Woodland Memorial Hospital, he lounged indolently on the cart. Her breath swooshed out of her lungs, only to be drawn back in with a sharp intake.

He'd looked arresting enough with clothes on, but now that she found herself staring eye to chest—bare chest—with this heart-stopping male, she was close to needing the defibrillator.

She'd seen patients in all stages of undress before. Why was this near-naked man having such an impact on her careening senses?

She moistened her lower lip and tried to breathe evenly. His shoulders were broad and beautiful, his chest muscle-hard and covered in dark curls. Her eyes followed its fleecy path with brazen fascination to where it disappeared beneath the sheet he held together at his waist. With the greatest effort, she forced her gaze upward to his face, meeting with a pair of eyes as green as a pine forest, flashing now with undisguised amusement as he observed her observing him.

"Would you like an eight-by-ten glossy?" His mouth broke into a flagrant grin as he struck a provocative centerfold pose, stretching his long lean body along the gurney for her easy perusal. "Color or black-and-white?"

Kyla felt her cheeks flame. She tried to speak, but nothing came out. She could only stand there, staring stupidly at him, praying for her hormones to return to their normal level of activity.

He wasn't overwhelmingly handsome—just compellingly attractive in an unsettling sort of way. His face was unabashedly sensual, punctuated by high angular cheekbones and a strong square chin. With his brown curly hair, those piercing green eyes, and that magnificent body, he looked as though he belonged in an ad for male underwear.

"Have I embarrassed you?" he asked.

He knew very well he had, and was thoroughly enjoying her discomfort. She met his penetrating gaze, longing to wipe the impudent expression off his face. But she couldn't. She had to continue to play the game she'd begun.

Wrenching her eyes away from him, she stared down into the bucket of disinfectant in front of her, forcing herself to concentrate on the scheme she'd concocted to give this overly nosy newsman what he deserved.

And she didn't have much time. Any moment now Roger would be having the zoo director paged.

"No, you didn't embarrass me," she replied emphatically, determined not to let him get the best of her. "I see lots around here." Then realizing how that must have sounded, she backpedaled. "I mean—"

He interrupted her attempt at an explanation with the quirk of one eyebrow and watched the color in her cheeks deepen to crimson. This sick-patient ruse was beginning to have advantages far more pleasant than just getting the jump on a story, he thought, observing the flutter of emotions that played across her striking features. A long lazy smile widened his mouth as he let his gaze trail over her burnished copper hair, her long neck, the swell of her breasts hidden beneath her striped top.

"I'll just bet you do see a lot around here, Miss . . . Grady," he said with a quick glance at the embroidered name on her smock. "*Mrs.* Grady," he corrected himself.

Damn! Just his luck—the girl was married. Somehow that surprised him. Married didn't fit her. She didn't seem like the kind of woman a man could tame easily. He sensed a certain spark of defiance in those stormy gray eyes, a certain rebelliousness of spirit in the tilt of her chin. But he had a story to write, he reminded himself. He wasn't here to seduce some young married woman with her hands in a cleaning bucket, no matter how soul-stirring she was. After all, he had his principles.

"I'll bet you not only see a lot around here, but hear a lot as well. In fact, I'd be willing to wager next month's salary that you know all about that donor heart that's due in here tonight."

This was Kyla's cue.

She turned her face upward to his and slipped easily into a role her high school drama teacher would have admired. She didn't feel a qualm of guilt. The man had it coming. "I don't know much," she began with staged deliberateness. "But I do know what I saw while I was mopping the hallway outside surgery a few minutes ago. . . ."

She watched him tense with eagerness, his eyes narrowed on her. "And what was that?"

"Well . . ." She paused, first faking a reluctance to go on, then meeting the questioning look on his face with all the theatrics she could command. "It was some of those people from the zoo—they brought in a . . . a baboon's heart."

Just then, the intercom crackled: "Jack Montana, Jack Montana, Extension 4070."

Kyla dared a sneak glance at her patsy. He'd recognized the zoo director's name all right! His eyes rounded to the size of golf balls. He'd bought the scam!

She allowed herself a hint of a satisfied smile as he tumbled off the gurney, his sheet dangling and twisting around his bare legs, like some scene out of a Woody Allen film. He battled to keep himself covered as he hopped around the room in search of his clothes. Kyla fought down a wave of laughter that threatened to give away the whole setup.

He found his belongings on the rack beneath the gurney, snatched them up and disappeared behind the folding screen in the corner. Seconds later he reappeared, not much more dressed than before. He was wearing his jeans, but his shirt flapped open, his socks stuck out of his back pocket, and he clutched his shoes to his chest.

Kyla barely had time to get out of his path before he bolted out of the treatment room and out the sliding glass doors of the ER.

In a state of stunned surprise, the staff watched him go, then shot Kyla a questioning look. "Where's he off to in such a hurry?"

Kyla shrugged. "Maybe the zoo to count the baboons—see if one of them is missing."

"Okay, Kyla, let's have it," Roger demanded. "What have you done?"

"Me? Why nothing. His curiosity did it all."

"You did something. Now, come on. Out with it."

She teased them with her reticence for a few moments more, then finally described the scenario, sending them into gales of laughter that left them hanging on to the nursing station desk for support. With the tension in the ER the past few days, it was what they'd all needed, a little foolishness, a little craziness.

"Wallace may very well demand your head on an intravenous pole for this," Roger said, when he could finally assemble the words. However, with tears coursing down his cheeks it was hard for Kyla to take his concern too seriously.

But as the staff's merriment continued to ring in her ears, Kyla glanced toward the glass doors of the ER. An odd sensation began to curl in the pit of her stomach— a tiny qualm of guilt. Had she been too hard on the guy?

IT WASN'T LONG BEFORE they heard the rhythmic chopping sounds of the helicopter. With surgery alerted, Kyla rushed outdoors to the helipad. The eggbeater blades were shutting down, their deafening noise fading into the fall night air. Two men raced toward her, hefting the foam container with its precious cargo. On the outside of it an orange label with bold black letters read Human Organ for Transplant.

Time was critical. The heart was imbedded in ice and chilled to four degrees Celsius, but it could not survive long outside the human body—four hours was the maximum.

"How are we doing on time, guys?" she asked.

"It's close."

She whisked them down the corridor to the operatory suite. Leonard Daniels was already being prepped in surgery. The blood and tissue matches were excellent. He had a chance. A good chance.

She watched the high drama through the glass window of Operating Room One. The surgical staff in pajamalike scrubs moved with a fluid grace. It gave her goose bumps to observe a surgery that, although commonplace these days, was one of the pioneering breakthroughs in medicine. She wondered if those grasping reporters ever felt anything akin to this as they stood at the scene of a breaking story. Somehow she doubted it. They were only out to scoop their competition, write a bigger headline—nothing more. With one last glance through the window, she wished Leonard Daniels well and then retreated down the hallway.

As the surgery doors swung wide to let her through, a mob from the press blocked her exit. Clamoring for a glimpse inside, they would have stampeded had it not been for the burly security guard stationed by the doorway. She recognized one or two of the more overly zealous newshounds who hung around the ER.

She searched the crowd for the brassy reporter who'd invaded the ER a short while before. She didn't see him. With his audacity he was probably inside, dressed in green scrubs, posing as one of the transplant team, she thought wryly.

Earlier, she'd pored over his patient file. He'd listed his name as Ted Spencer, his age: thirty-five; marital status: single; weight: one-ninety-five; height: six-foot-two, and sex: *yeah!* She'd been unable to resist a smile at the guy's sense of humor.

As she tried to make her way through the throng of reporters, the group descended on her, pelting her with questions. "What's going on in there?" "Where did the heart come from?" they demanded.

She considered telling them it came from South America—the heart of a Nazi war criminal, but she resisted the impulse. If that got into the papers, Wallace *would* have her head on an IV pole!

"Come on, Bradford," one persisted. "Give us a statement."

"Go chase an ambulance, Merkle," she retorted. Ralph Merkle was one of the worst. She negotiated an end run around him before he could recover from her remark.

As she neared the ER she saw Ted Spencer outside the double doors talking animatedly with Mrs. Grady, the real Mrs. Grady. Desperately, she looked for a doorway to duck into. After just tangling with Merkle and his bloodthirsty pack of reporters, she was not anxious for another confrontation with a member of the press, especially not this one.

But it was too late; Mrs. Grady had spotted her.

"Miss Bradford, will you please tell this man who I am? He doesn't believe me," the housekeeping aide lamented.

Ted Spencer's head swiveled toward Kyla, his eyes locking with hers. As recognition flooded his face, his mouth hardened into a grim straight line.

"Yes, Miss Kyla Bradford, R.N." He read the name tag pinned to the front of her lab coat. "And while you're at it, perhaps you'd like to explain why you moonlight as a cleaning woman!"

"Well, if it isn't Mr. Spencer." She straightened her willowy frame to a defiant five-foot-eight. "I hardly recognized you with your clothes on!"

Actually, he was magnificent with his clothes on or off. The recollection of how he'd looked wearing nothing but a sheet in the treatment room flashed into her mind, sending small shivery sensations up her spine.

"Look, I'm covering an important story here," he said, planting his hands on his hips, and spacing his feet wide apart. "But you want to play games—not that I actually believed that crazy charade of yours."

She'd made a fool of him earlier, and from the looks of him, he didn't like it one bit. "Oh, you believed it all right. And what do you mean, I play games? What gives you the right to masquerade as a patient in a busy hospital, wasting the time of valuable personnel?"

In one unexpected motion his hands flew forward, grasping her shoulders. Suddenly, his size and power made her feel the weaker combatant. She took a step backward and met with the hard surface of the corridor wall. Every nerve in her body tensed. She felt the heat in his hands through the fabric of her uniform, his touch electrifying her from head to toe.

He leaned close, his face so near she could feel the warm tingle of his breath against her cheek. The raw masculine scent of his after-shave tickled her nostrils. "I take advantage of any source I can, anytime I can," he said, his voice low and deep.

The cool green of his eyes traced the outline of her lips, and for one breathtaking, completely unsettling moment Kyla thought he was going to kiss her. Not an altogether unpleasant thought, she realized, trying to quiet down her heart racing at triple-time. Instead, he loosened his grip on her and she broke free.

What right did he have to be so upset? He'd invaded *her* Emergency Room. All she'd done was expose him for the imposter he was.

"It's too bad Dr. Mason didn't remove your appendix," she shot back at him, finding her voice at last. "But that would have given you a front row seat in surgery. You'd have liked that just fine, wouldn't you? Tell me, just how far would you go for a story, Mr. Spencer?"

"To the fiery brink of hell if I have to, lady." His voice was steely and intense, making her pulse race faster. She had never felt such a strong physical attraction to a man before. But Ted Spencer, in his rumpled corduroy jacket and slim tight jeans, was having a decided effect on her.

"You have no qualms about lying your way into the Emergency Room?" She tried to focus her anger, anger that kept getting derailed.

"None whatsoever. I consider it innovative journalism."

"I consider it deceitful, dishonest and—"

"Excuse me," Mrs. Grady interrupted, leaning wearily on the handle of her mop. They'd both completely forgotten her in the heat of their vehement debate. "Could you two move your argument over to the other side of the hall. As soon as I finish mopping this floor I can go home, and I'd like very much to go home."

"Don't worry, Mrs. Grady. This argument is finished," Ted replied evenly, not taking his hostile eyes off Kyla's face.

"Yes. Mr. Spencer has a story to write. I wouldn't want to stand in the way of innovative journalism," Kyla said sarcastically, returning his glowering look.

He turned and walked away. A muttered oath escaped his lips as he strode down the hospital corridor without a backward glance, his footsteps heavy in the tiled hall.

"If I ever see that man again, it will be one day too soon," Kyla announced.

DURING THE FOLLOWING WEEK, the tale of how Kyla made a monkey out of the reporter grew to legendary proportions. It was told and retold until the story bore little resemblance to the actual incident. Only when the parking lot attendant recounted his version of the story to Wallace Osgood as he was parking his car, did it fail to get a laugh.

At first the administrator didn't believe it. It was too absurd to be true. But everywhere he went in the hospital, he heard the story in one form or another.

Kyla was upset that the incident had spread through the grapevine like crabgrass in August. She confronted the group she worked with, demanding to know which one of them had the flappy jaw.

"Ah, come on, Kyla," Roger said. "This story was just too rich to keep to ourselves. I'm sorry it got out of hand, though. But you have to admit, even the exaggerations are funny."

"Not to me, they're not," she retorted, hurt that Roger, her friend, had been involved in the rumors. But he *had* tried to stop her. If word of it had reached Wallace's ears she had only herself to blame, she knew.

It wasn't long before Kyla was summoned to Wallace's office. Her superior sat very still behind his desk, looking like rigor mortis had set in, waiting for her to squirm. She wouldn't give him the satisfaction.

"You were told not to speak to reporters," he began, his voice full of the suppressed rage that was so much worse than the outright kind. "You were not to give out any information whatsoever, much less blatantly false information. If even a hint of this wild story had hit the papers, every animal rights group in the country would have been camped out in this hospital, and we would have had to spend a lot of time and money denying the allegations—not taking into account the bad publicity we would have received." Wallace went on and on with his lecture.

Kyla knew he was right. She got what she deserved, but she had the feeling the administrator would make her wish she'd never laid eyes on Ted Spencer.

Then something Wallace was saying brought her back to the present with a start. "No, sir, I did not dress up in a monkey costume and stalk the surgery hallway. There are more than fourteen absurd versions of this incident running rampant through the hospital. You know they couldn't all be true."

"That's just the point, Miss Bradford. They are running rampant through the hospital. Didn't you foresee the consequences of your little charade?"

"But there's really no damage done. It'll all soon be forgotten. I don't see..." Kyla stopped, noticing the vein bulge in his neck. She knew she had pushed him about as far as she dared.

"One more incident," he said, shaking a warning finger at her, "one more incident of any sort, and I'll be forced to take punitive action against you."

Kyla met his look and realized he meant every word he said. This was all so unfair. Although it had been a harebrained trick to pull on Ted Spencer, the man deserved it. However, Wallace was in no mood to listen. She swallowed the rebuttal she'd been about to make.

"Do we see eye to eye on this?"

He expected an affirmative answer, and wanting to get out of his office, Kyla gave him one.

"Now that we have that settled, I have a request to make of you." The tone of his voice indicated it would be more of an order. "The *Courier* wants to do a feature on this hospital. We're big time now that we've done a successful heart transplant. People will want to know about us. And favorable publicity always pleases our venerable board of directors." He gave a short laugh.

Kyla shifted about in her seat, wondering what any of this had to do with her.

"Miss Bradford, I want you to show the press around, not just in Emergency, but in all the services."

Kyla was out of her chair in a flash. "But we have a PR person to handle all that. You don't need me—"

Wallace put up a hand to silence her. "Violet is going to be out at least another week—her father is quite ill. I've been trying to handle the publicity myself throughout Leonard Daniels's surgery, but frankly, I don't have the time to do any more. I'll brief the reporter in the morning, but I want you to handle the tour."

"I'm sure there must be someone on your staff who . . ." she began, searching for some way to convince him to change his mind.

Wallace rose to his feet behind his desk. "Miss Bradford, you seemed to have developed quite an interest lately in informing the press of what this hospital is doing. Let's see if we can turn that interest into something . . . constructive for a change."

Kyla gasped. "Is this supposed to be a punishment, Wallace?"

"Punishment? No, although if it was, it would be most fitting. The fact is, with Violet out I really do need your help."

Kyla bit her lower lip to keep from speaking. Perhaps he did need her help. One thing she knew for sure—no way would Wallace accept a refusal from her. It might not be too bad, she told herself. He would do the preliminaries. She'd show the reporter through the various departments, let the department heads discuss the details, and it would be over. She'd keep it brief, impersonal and strictly professional.

At least the reporter wouldn't be Ted Spencer, she thought with a private smile. He wouldn't be able to show his face around the hospital again. The stories circulating about him made him look like a first-class clown.

"All right, Wallace. I'll do it," she said quietly.

2

"IT'S TURTLE TIME ALONG I-35, folks. Watch out for the orange and white barrels near the downtown loop."

Kyla reached over and clicked off her car radio. "Tell me about it!" she groaned, as she maneuvered her battered blue Mustang around the road construction that had reduced traffic to a veritable crawl. "And it's not even rush hour!"

At times like this, she longed for the simplicity of her sleepy little hometown, buried in the rolling Missouri hills. Lewistown, with its thirty-bed hospital and no traffic snarl-ups, no congestion of any kind—unless she counted the time her father's flatbed trailer overturned on the railroad tracks, spilling the load of apples and peaches he was taking to the farmers' market. It had stopped traffic in both directions until the 8:10 came highballing through and made fruit compote out of his produce.

The memory brought a smile to her lips. Home. The apple orchard with its smattering of peach trees. The large white house where she'd grown up. Its nurturing warmth, its solitude always beckoned her back. At rough times in her life she'd been tempted to return. But

Kansas City was home now—in spite of the fact that the freeway traffic sometimes resembled a parking lot.

Kyla took a quick glance at her watch. If this logjam of cars didn't move soon, she was going to be late. Wallace had ordered her to come in at noon to handle the interview with the newspaper reporter. She let out a sigh. There was nothing to do but settle back and try to relax while easing her car forward half a car length at a time.

The downtown skyline was visible in the distance, pearly gray against the vivid blue backdrop of the sky. It was one of those rare fall days that inspire poets—and TV weathermen. A crisp breeze fluttered through the open car window, ruffling the rebellious wisps of Kyla's hair that refused to be caught up into her practical off-the-collar twist. She smoothed away a wrinkle her seat belt was threatening to press into the skirt of her fresh uniform.

Why wouldn't this traffic move?

In an attempt to ease her frustration, she flipped the car radio back on, her index finger jabbing at the buttons until she found music suitable for a jammed interstate. But even the strains from her favorite easy listening station did little to quell her impatience.

It was ten minutes past twelve when she pulled into the employee parking lot. Wallace would be in a real snit, she thought, as she searched for a space. When the last row failed to yield a spot, she created her own on the bright yellow stripes indicating the walkway to the building. The Mustang fit perfectly, with just enough room to spare for pedestrians, she decided. Her day was beginning to improve!

She waved a greeting to Clarence, buffing the hallway with his giant silver machine. Clarence nodded and flashed her a smile as she headed off in the direction of the administrative wing. If time permitted in the afternoon, she wanted to make a stop at Coronary Care and say a brief hello to Leonard Daniels, who was finally allowed a few visitors. Kyla had checked on his progress daily, worrying along with his nurses those first critical days. So far, he showed no sign of rejecting his new heart, but as they all knew, the subsequent weeks would tell the real tale.

The press was kept away, a rule strictly enforced, until such time as Mr. Daniels felt up to granting an interview, and then, only if his doctors were in agreement.

The door to Wallace Osgood's office was ajar, so Kyla rapped once and pushed her way in. "Wallace, I'm sorry I'm . . ." Her voice stalled as her gaze fastened on the visitor seated across from the administrator. Wearing a satisfied smirk and with very little charity in his eyes, Ted Spencer rose from his chair and nodded at her. "Sorry I'm late," she somehow managed to finish. At that moment she wished she were someplace else, anyplace else.

The Fates were clearly not smiling on her. As Ted's gaze traveled slowly over her, she took a deep measured breath and forced herself to remain calm, resisting the urge to adjust the buttons on the front of her uniform or brush back a strand of hair. She refused to give him the edge by these self-conscious gestures. Instead, she turned her attention to the man standing beside him.

He was obviously Ted's cameraman, a thin wraith with cameras and other paraphernalia hanging from him, as if they were strange appendages. His hair was wild and red. Thick spectacles magnified his blue eyes to the size of giant marbles as he shuffled impatiently in his sandals and ragged jeans. He wore one of those T-shirts that make a statement—I'm a Party Animal, this one said.

Before Kyla could form a judgment about whom he might possibly find to party with, her thoughts were interrupted by Wallace Osgood. "I'm glad you could finally make it, Miss Bradford," he said with an equal mixture of sarcasm and peevishness.

"Wallace, I'm truly sorry, but the road construction—"

He raised a hand, indicating he did not wish to hear her excuse. "I'd like you to meet the man you'll be working with—Mr. Ted Spencer. One of the *Courier's* top journalists. We're most fortunate to have him with us today."

From his introduction it was apparent Wallace did not know that this was the very reporter she'd duped so notoriously a week earlier. She cast a quick glance at Ted. He fixed her with a wry smile, his green eyes regarding her with restrained amusement, but he said nothing. She acknowledged his presence with a stiff nod of her head. She could not have spoken even if she'd had to. The moisture in her mouth had dried up and her tongue felt as if it was tied in a granny knot.

"And this is his photographer," Wallace went on. "Mr . . . er . . . Blood Hound."

"The name's really Cunningham, miss. But all my friends call me Blood Hound for obvious reasons." Blood Hound began shooting pictures of her from every angle, dozens of them.

Ted was clearly enjoying the situation, watching her squirm under the unrelenting snaps of the shutter. He made no move to stop his trigger-happy cameraman.

Kyla felt her composure slipping. "Is this necessary?" She fired the question directly at Ted rather than at Blood Hound, feeling it was his place to control his overzealous photographer.

Finally Ted motioned Blood Hound's camera into submission.

"Sorry about that," Blood Hound said. "I get carried away when I see a pretty face."

Kyla fought to steady her nerves.

"I have to admit the guy has good taste," Ted murmured, appraising her in a way that robbed her of breath.

She chided herself for her ridiculous reaction to him and ordered her respiration to return to normal. Instead, she should be trying to decide how she was going to get through this interview and still keep her sanity intact.

Wallace Osgood cleared his throat loudly, bringing everyone's attention back to the matter at hand. "I hope I've been helpful and I haven't bored you with too many dull facts about this institution." He smiled affably at Ted.

Ted smiled back, but wisely said nothing.

"Now I'll turn you over to Miss Bradford," the administrator continued. "I daresay you'll find her far more interesting. Ahem! Her portion of the interview, that is," he added, but not before Ted could cast an anticipatory leer in Kyla's direction.

Kyla groaned faintly, then followed the pair out of the office. Once she was out of the administrator's earshot, she turned all her fury on Ted. "You planned this!"

"No, actually I didn't. But it couldn't have worked out better if I had. I can make you look like a fool in this article, Miss Bradford, or a veritable Florence Nightingale, which you definitely are not."

Kyla dug her nails into her palms to control her fury. Ted Spencer might have the upper hand for the moment, but she did not intend to let him keep it. If she had to do this interview, she fully intended to be the one controlling it.

"Shall we begin?" she suggested sweetly.

Ted nodded his consent, then followed her down the hallway. His hand found the small of her back as he guided her through the maze of staff and visitors.

His light touch, the warmth of his fingers through her uniform, held her prisoner for a moment longer than they should have. Startled by her response, she pulled away, reminding herself she should keep a safe distance. He was an unprincipled reporter who'd not only lied his way into the ER but who'd just threatened to make her look like a fool in his newspaper.

Blood Hound was snapping pictures of everyone walking along the corridor. His subjects cast puzzled looks in Kyla's direction or hurried on, obviously disconcerted by a camera recording their movements in successive flashes.

Finally Kyla had enough. "I want you to call off the shutterbug," she flared. "Your paper may supply him with endless rolls of film, but this is a hospital, and it would do you both good to bear that in mind."

"You're right, of course," Ted conceded. "Blood Hound, down boy!" he said, corralling his photographer. He took him aside, adding in a loud whisper, "We're upsetting the nice lady."

Kyla clenched her fists at her sides. The man was incorrigible!

"We're ready now. He says he'll behave."

Kyla shook her head wearily.

"Where first?" Ted gave her an eager look.

Kyla had been trying to decide just that. There was the morgue, but a squeamish shudder ran through her at the thought.

"This way," she said, and they fell into step behind a dietary worker pushing a metal cart, following him right into the diet kitchen. "We'll begin here," she said and watched Ted's face fall when he looked around.

She relished the look of boredom on it even more as she explained in great detail what constituted a bland diet and a surgical liquid. She noted—with a certain glee—that he wrote none of these fascinating facts down in the reporter's notebook he carried.

She continued her spiel over the clatter of dishes, ignoring his inattention. Blood Hound contented himself with snapping pictures of the trays that skimmed along the large black conveyor belt.

Midway through the rounds of the hospital's laundry facilities, Ted's impatience boiled over. "This is the sort of tour you'd take a pack of Cub Scouts on. You know I don't want to see this stuff. How about showing me around surgery?"

"Surgery?" Why didn't that surprise her?

And then the idea came to her. She'd give Ted Spencer just what he'd asked for.

"Okay, surgery it is—but I can't have Blood Hound in there taking pictures. Maybe later, when the schedule's finished," she half promised, anxious to get rid of the maniacal cameraman who didn't fit into her little scheme.

Reluctantly Ted agreed to her condition. He sent his photographer off to have a cup of coffee in the cafeteria, telling him he'd catch up to him later.

Blood Hound ambled away, and Kyla hoped he'd find no one to terrorize with his camera in the interim. Dismissing him from her mind, she led Ted off in the direction of the surgical wing.

She couldn't help noticing the admiring glances he got from the female staff they passed. *Some women will be impressed by anything!* she thought with rising annoyance. His wide shoulders did pad his rumpled corduroy sports jacket nicely, she had to admit as her gaze flickered lightly over him. His skintight jeans hugged his lower torso, revealing athletically muscular legs and a great tush. A rather well-put-together piece of protoplasm, she conceded, but *I'm not buying.* Quickly she averted her eyes before he could notice her covert appraisal of him.

"Tell me about Kyla Bradford, R.N.," he said as they walked along the hallway. If he was aware of the passing stares, he gave no indication.

"Are you trying to interview me, Mr. Spencer?" she asked, eyes narrowing.

"Maybe."

He was studying her intently, which made her feel uncomfortable. He had nice eyes, intelligent, unsettling . . . sexy eyes.

"Maybe I just want to know more about the lady who runs Emergency with an iron hand."

Kyla's uneasiness increased and she looked away. "For your article, I suppose." What was he up to?

"Woodland's Emergency Room has the reputation of being the best in the city. I've heard you're the main reason for that reputation."

Kyla's eyes flashed to his. A compliment? Or just his way of buttering her up? "It has the reputation because we all work hard. And we care—every last one of us." Let him put that in his newspaper.

He smiled down at her. It was an engaging smile that didn't look in any way deceitful. Still, she was on her guard.

"And what about off duty? Is there a man in your life?" He lifted one dark eyebrow questioningly at her.

Kyla felt a prickle of irritation. Her love life, or lack thereof, was no concern of his. "If we have to do this interview, let's keep it on a professional level. Okay?"

"You can't blame me for being inquisitive," he reasoned, his smile widening into a teasing grin. "After all, it's my business to ask questions."

"But I'm not the focus of this article. It's the hospital and what it has to offer the community. That is the point of your story, isn't it?" She tried to bring him back to the matter at hand. Somehow, just his asking the question put their association on a more intimate footing—and that was the last thing she wanted with this man.

"I was only trying to get to know you. Is there anything wrong with that?" The soft lights in his eyes and the hypnotic smile playing at his lips said there wasn't, making her temporarily doubt her own mind.

"Yes . . . no . . . I mean . . ." She couldn't think of a single reason at the moment but she didn't doubt that there were plenty. She stopped walking and fixed him with a stern look. "Like I said, let's keep this strictly professional. Okay?"

"Why?" He ran a finger along the curve of her cheek, stopping at the indentation in her chin. "Are you afraid you might find you like me, Kyla Bradford?"

Kyla moistened her lower lip, fighting back the odd sensation of heat suffusing her body. "Fat chance," she returned, not wanting to admit even the possibility. She turned and walked on.

Ted followed, catching up to her easily. "You don't care much for reporters, do you?"

"To put it bluntly, I don't. Especially pushy reporters who lie and deceive their way into the ER for the sake of a story."

"All's fair in love, war and journalism, Miss Bradford."

All's fair in guided tours, too, Mr. Spencer, Kyla thought to herself.

They had reached the surgical observation room. Kyla remembered seeing the surgery Roger would perform listed on the chalkboard last night before she went home. She saw his familiar green-garbed frame busy below them. The surgery had already begun—the removal of a bullet from the leg of a liquor store assailant. Nothing critical, but definitely bloody. And perfect for her purposes. All's fair, Mr. Spencer, she thought again, a smile tilting at her lips.

The observation room was crowded with residents because Roger was demonstrating a new surgical technique. She led Ted to a seat with a good view of the scene below.

"The patient has a bullet lodged in his right thigh near the bone." Kyla explained the circumstances of the case to Ted. "It did extensive damage with its entry. Dr. Mason is attempting to remove it, clean away all the damaged tissue, then close." Patches of crimson on the blue-green sterile towels that draped the operative field began to widen. Roger fought coolly to clamp off the bleeders.

"Some of these operations aren't very pretty. I hope you can take it—all this blood, I mean." It was a calculated statement.

She waited for him to reply that he was tough or something equally macho, but when no response came she glanced over at him. Beads of moisture dotted his forehead and upper lip. His skin had taken on a dead pallor and his eyes had lost their deep luster.

"Spencer, I think you've seen enough," she said, realizing her strategy had worked beautifully, and in record time. But to make him endure any more would be too cruel.

He shrugged out of his jacket and tossed it beside him. "No, I'm fine," he insisted.

Roger's voice came through the intercom, explaining the debriding technique for the benefit of the students. It was a very graphic description. Kyla glanced at Ted once again. His face rivaled her uniform for whiteness.

"Come on, I'm getting you out of here," she said.

He brushed a shirt sleeve across his perspiring forehead. "I'm all right."

The next moment he folded like the morning newspaper and slid to the floor just as quietly.

Before Kyla could make a move, three residents jumped up and carried Ted's limp body out of the room. She'd never meant for things to go this far. She'd only wanted to hear him beg for mercy, not collapse at her feet.

"Kyla, what in thunder's going on up there?" It was Roger's voice booming through the intercom.

"Some wimp couldn't take it," one of the residents answered, and the room broke into howls.

Kyla whirled on the heckler. "Ah, Nolan, I think I remember hearing that they had to carry you out once, too."

The room exploded into laughter again.

She hurried out, finding that they had carried Ted into a small lounge across the hall.

"Get him a drink of water or something," Nolan said from over her shoulder. "He looks green enough to plant."

Someone came in with a cool cloth, and Kyla pressed it to Ted's forehead. Slowly his skin began to regain some of its color, and she felt relief seep back into her tensed body. She was not proud of what she'd done to this man. There was something reprehensible about bringing a big man so low. Half sprawled on the couch, he looked nothing like the arrogant reporter who'd invaded the ER a week earlier.

All was not fair in love and war, she decided. Sometimes things went too far.

She drew her hand away from the cloth and gently stroked his cheek. Smooth skin gave way to rough as she felt a faint bristle of beard beneath the tips of her fingers. Lightly she brushed his lips, tracing their outline. He had the most incredible mouth. Full and sensuous, almost pouting—except when he smiled. She liked it when he smiled, but she hadn't given him much reason to do that lately, she thought with a swift stab of guilt.

Ted groaned and moved slightly. He reached for his head, found the cool cloth and yanked it off. Opening his eyes he looked dazedly around the room as if trying to get his bearings. Four pairs of eyes stared at him, three belonging to strangers, the fourth pair to Kyla. It was to this wide gray set that he directed his glower and his words.

"Do you get some kind of perverse pleasure out of putting me at a disadvantage, lady?" His voice was as cold as a Kansas City winter.

"He's all yours, Kyla," the residents said before fleeing.

"Thanks a lot, guys." Her voice was tinged with sarcasm.

Ted tried to sit up.

Kyla grabbed his upper arms, feeling the steely muscles flex beneath her fingers. "Stay down, Ted. Give your blood pressure a chance to stabilize."

"If I stay down, you'll probably give me poison next."

He shoved her aside and sat up. The room spun crazily. He put his hands to his head and flopped back against the cushions of the couch.

Kyla touched his shoulder and felt the tension coil in him. "I didn't mean for this to happen," she said.

A scowl enveloped his features. "Don't expect me to believe that one. I don't know what it is you have against reporters, but I'm sure as hell not going to stick around to find out."

He got to his feet, visibly wobbling.

"Don't be so stubborn. Let me help you," she said, placing an arm around his waist. Again she felt the tension knot in him.

He spun around to face her. Green fire lit his eyes. "I think you've done quite enough for one day." With that he sailed out of the room with as much dignity as he could muster.

THE NEWSROOM WAS NO MORE A ZOO than usual that afternoon. It just seemed that way to Ted, who was fighting both his anger at Kyla Bradford and the after-effects of fainting—the second acute embarrassment he'd suffered at her hands.

She was a real viper. Whoever had granted her a nursing degree was a sadist. Putting his hands together and glancing heavenward, he prayed, "Dear God, if I'm ever sick give me a painful death rather than nursing at the hands of that woman."

She gives angel of mercy a whole new meaning, he thought as he continued to pound out his story on his computer terminal. His notes were scattered over his desk in one giant mosaic, the facts and figures Wallace Osgood had supplied him with. He'd gotten very little from Miss Bradford except a headache and a bad taste in his mouth for the nursing profession.

He took a long swig of coffee before realizing it was cold. It slopped over his notes when he returned the mug to his desk. He shoved the remains of a brick-hard sugar doughnut off a napkin and dabbed at the brown liquid in a half-hearted attempt to soak it up.

Ripping his story off the printer he read it over hurriedly. What he read told him he'd let his opinion of one gray-eyed, copper-haired nurse color the article. Sprinkled in among the salient facts of the piece were sharp comments about the staff at Woodland, the questionable ethics of a nurse who used surgery and the Emergency Room as the setting for her jokes and little pranks, and an administrator who allowed this sort of behavior in his hospital. It contradicted everything he'd heard beforehand about Kyla Bradford and her ER's sterling reputation.

And he knew he couldn't print it!

With a groan he started to wad up the article and toss it in the wastebasket, then realized that the story was actually there. He would just delete his own unprintable, albeit justifiable, feelings and file it before tonight's deadline. But first he had to have fresh coffee. The fainting episode earlier had left him feeling strange, just on the edge of lightheaded. He laid the article on his desk and fished in his pocket for some quarters.

His steps faltered as he reached the alcove housing the various vending machines that kept the *Courier's* staff from dehydration and starvation. Maybe a candy bar to counteract the shakiness, he thought, as he fumbled for more change.

"Hey, Spence," Blood Hound greeted him. "What gives? You don't look so hot. I just developed the hospital pictures. Wanna see 'em?"

"Later, Blood Hound. Pick out the best shots and lay them on my desk with my article." He lowered his head to ward off the fuzzy feeling and disappeared toward the parking lot.

As soon as he stepped outside, the fresh air began to revive him. He eased his tall frame into his silver Porsche, the only extravagance he'd allowed himself from the family money, and snapped his seat belt around him.

He would grab a quick take-out from Arthur Bryant's, his favorite barbecue restaurant, and catch a short nap at his apartment before returning to the paper to edit the hospital article into something printable. At least the original version had been a great catharsis, a vent for his smoldering anger.

A short while later, he pulled up in front of his midtown apartment and maneuvered the sports car into a tight space between two parked cars. The brown paper sack containing his take-out lay on the seat beside him. Bryant's had the best barbecue in four states. He could already taste the savory beef—along with the last remaining bottle of beer he had in his foodless refrigerator. The prefect thing to wash down the bad taste he had in his mouth for Kyla Bradford.

He snatched up his dinner and took the stairs to his third-floor apartment, two at a time. He wasn't going to get steamed up over her again! Never in his life had he fainted—not even when he'd been knifed on assignment down in the tenderloin several years ago, doing that feature on the homeless. He massaged the old wound on his thigh, remembering the pain.

Fainting was such a weakness. The memory of this afternoon's incident galled him—as did the realization that this project was a three-part series. He would have to spend more time at Woodland before he could complete the assignment, the assignment he regretfully remembered he'd begged his editor to give him. And all

because he'd wanted the chance to see one tempes-
tuous ER nurse again.

He turned the key in the lock and entered his apartment. Strangely, the clutter of the place calmed him. It
was all his, even though it upset his family that he could
live like this when he'd been used to more palatial sur-
roundings. He found the bottle of beer in the refrigerator, then shoved a pile of unfolded laundry off the
couch and sank back against the cushions to enjoy his
barbecue and watch the evening news. The strange
feeling in his head began to disappear. Maybe he'd just
been hungry.

When the news was over, he watched the Wheel and
enjoyed the curves of the game show hostess's body as
she paraded back and forth across the stage, turning the
giant letters. He felt himself relax. The beer was making him drowsy.

His eyelids flickered, then closed.

Apartment sounds woke him—a gurgle of water
through the ancient pipes, the slam of a door. He
opened his eyes to a garish white light, then realized it
was his TV hissing electronic snow across its screen.

What time was it? He started as his body uncramped
itself from its sleeping position. Geez! It was morning!
His deadline . . .

Ten minutes later Ted was in his car, heading downtown. Twenty minutes later he pulled into his parking
stall at the *Courier*. Never before had he missed a

deadline—that spitfire at the hospital was turning his life upside down!

From habit he snatched a copy of the morning edition from a table in the newsroom as he made his way in, one excuse and then another forming on his lips.

"Spencer, this is one steamy first-parter you wrote on the hospital assignment," Riley, one of the staff reporters, chuckled as he looked up from his copy of the paper.

Ted stopped mid-stride, gave Riley a questioning look, then ripped the paper from his hands. "What first-parter?"

The newsprint swam before his eyes, but he was able to focus on enough of the article to realize that this was his unedited story in black and white.

3

KYLA HEARD VOICES. First her own, then another. She heard the faraway sound of ringing, like a telephone, then the voices again. Her sleep-fogged mind struggled to understand what was happening.

"The answering machine." She gave a protesting groan. Her eyelids fluttered a few times, her eyes trying to adjust to the bright sunlight filtering through the slats of the miniblinds at her bedroom window. She groaned again, burrowing her head beneath the pillow to block out everything but the peaceful cocoon of darkness and silence.

But the ringing continued, followed by the voices. She'd never heard her answering machine that busy! What was going on? Fire? Flood? A shoe sale at Timothy's? Whatever it was, she didn't want to know.

She'd been awake half the night, nursing her conscience. Remorse and regret had kept her company, as well, and they were still exacting their penance this morning. Her head thumped as if it had a pulse beat all its own. When she thought of what she'd done to Spencer, she wasn't very proud of herself.

From beneath the insulation of the pillow, she heard the machine activate once more. She hoped it wasn't

Roger again. He had called last night, offering her a hefty piece of his mind about the idiocy of bringing that reporter in to view such a bloody surgery. Hadn't she realized the poor sucker was bound to keel over? Her third-rate Laurel and Hardy routine had turned the Operating Room into a circus, he'd chided.

Roger's censure had succeeded in making her feel worse, something she hadn't thought possible. She'd admitted the lunacy of the whole episode and had apologized to him. She hadn't meant to disrupt surgery. She'd only wanted to give one slick reporter his comeuppance. But her plan had backfired, leaving her looking like the horse's behind.

Kyla let out a ragged sigh. Enough self-reproach. It wasn't changing anything. What was done was done. She pulled her head out from under the pillow and scrutinized the clock on the table beside her bed. It was noon. Time to get up and face the day.

The bold, bright-flowered sheets were pulled loose at the foot of the bed, giving eloquent testimony to her night of fitful sleep. The quilted spread lay in a heap on the floor where she'd kicked it off during the night. She found her faded terry robe among the covers and pulled it on, wrapping it snugly around her for solace.

She didn't have to be at the hospital until two-thirty. There was time for a late breakfast and a play-through of her morning messages, she thought, as she struggled to put Ted Spencer and the ill-fated consequences of yesterday afternoon out of her mind. It was better to adopt a philosophical attitude about it all and get on with life, she decided.

She stretched her limbs like a sleek cat, then padded barefoot across the hardwood floor through the living room and into the kitchen. Her main objective was coffee—strong and black.

Kyla lived over the garage in a small carriage house, tucked away behind a gray stone mansion in one of Kansas City's fine old neighborhoods. In more gracious times it had been the carriage driver's living quarters, then later, with the advent of the automobile, the chauffeur's.

It had sat empty for years, abandoned and forgotten, until Kyla had found it and begged the owner to rent it to her. She'd spent two months sanding floors, patching walls and staining woodwork until her hands resembled tree bark. When she was finished she'd refashioned it into a cozy apartment, decorated with warm antiques and hanging plants.

Brushing her thick tousled hair back from her face, she flipped on her answering machine and set about making coffee. Leah's voice came on first. "Kyla, have you read this morning's *Courier*? Check out page three."

It must be a shoe sale at Timothy's, she thought, spooning several scoops of coffee into the brewing basket.

She dropped two slices of bread into the toaster as the next message came on, this one from Allie, another nurse who often worked the ER with her. "Kyla, seen the *Courier*? Take a look on page three."

Must be quite a sale. Both of her friends knew the penchant she had for buying shoes. She got the butter and strawberry preserves out of the refrigerator.

The next message was from Wallace, sounding like he'd had something sour for breakfast. "Miss Bradford, can't you answer your telephone? I hate these confounded machines. Get back to me and quick!"

That was definitely not about a shoe sale!

Kyla hurried downstairs to retrieve the morning edition from outside her door, then retraced her steps. With the paper tucked under her arm, she carried her toast and coffee to the kitchen table and settled into a ladder-back chair. "Page three, hmm."

She scanned the page and then she saw it—the hospital article with Ted Spencer's byline slashed across the page. An involuntary gasp escaped her lips as she read, her eyes rounding in stunned disbelief.

"How could he . . . ?"

The article cast aspersions not only on her and the rest of the ER nursing staff but on the hospital as well. And he'd portrayed Wallace as a perfect fool, if not a total incompetent. The man might have his inadequacies but he didn't deserve this, she thought defensively.

She crumpled the page in her tight fists and then ripped it into pieces. If Spencer had wanted to get even with her, did he have to hurt others in the process? Fighting back tears of rage she flung the torn remnants onto the kitchen table, almost sending her coffee cup crashing to the floor.

She furrowed her fingers through her hair and paced back and forth across the kitchen. How dare he get his revenge on her in so base a way—involving the hospital and its staff, involving Wallace.

Wallace!

She stopped her nervous pacing and sank into a kitchen chair, suddenly weak in the knees. That's what Wallace had called about. He'd read the *Courier*, seen the article. She had to talk to him, to explain.

Explain what? How? What could she possibly say that would get her hide out of the fire this time? With a defeated groan, she dropped her head into her hands.

KYLA SMOOTHED AN IMAGINARY WRINKLE from the skirt of her uniform and straightened her collar before rapping on the door of the administrator's office. She forced back her shoulders and lifted her chin determinedly.

She had no real defense and she knew it. Wallace had every right to be angry with her. She'd failed him, the hospital, the staff—all because she'd let one wretched reporter get to her.

Pushing open the door, she stepped inside and positioned herself in front of her superior's primly arranged desk. "You wanted to see me?"

"Sit down, Miss Bradford." She could tell by the cold calm in his voice that she didn't have a prayer.

FIFTEEN MINUTES LATER the session mercifully ended. Wallace had been unforgiving and grim as he handed down her stiff punishment. Suspension from work—three days. What had she expected from him? More than a slap on the wrist, certainly—but this?

Ted Spencer had baited her beautifully, and she hadn't even seen it coming. He played rough, way out of her league. But then, he had warned her. Kyla remembered his words: "I can make you look like a fool in this article, Miss Bradford, or a veritable Florence Nightingale, which you definitely are not." Well, she and Florence had very little in common at the moment.

Kyla escaped Wallace's office and fled into the hallway. All she wanted to do was get away before the tears welling up in her eyes spilled over. She'd only made it two yards from the administrator's door when she heard her name called. Kyla recognized the voice; the last time she'd heard it, it had been full of anger.

Now the anger was all hers and that anger forestalled her tears. Ted Spencer had managed to make her look like a fool, but she would not give him the satisfaction of seeing her cry.

"Out of my way, Spencer," she said as her long strides carried her down the hall. She tried to shove past him, but he caught her arm and whirled her to a stop.

"I came to explain. To Osgood . . . and to you."

His eyes locked with hers, holding them like a magnet. His fingers were warm on her skin, exerting a pressure more perceived than actual. Kyla's breath caught and she cursed herself for her involuntary reaction to him. Even in her anger, the man had an impact on her. She swallowed against the tight knot of fury in her throat and pulled her arm free from his grasp.

"Explain! I hardly think that's possible."

"Kyla, this whole thing was a misunderstanding."

She tipped her face up to his, her eyes narrowing. "A misunderstanding? Is that what you're calling it?" He had mousetrapped her, plain and simple. Having heard enough, she turned to leave.

"Kyla, wait!" He stepped forward, blocking her retreat, trapping her against the wall, an arm on either side of her.

Kyla gave an exasperated shrug. "You've got me, Spencer. Now what are you going to do with me?"

Ted looked down at her taunting smile. He knew what he wanted to do with her. He wanted to kiss every trace of mockery off of her lips. He wanted to feel them soften under his, to part in invitation, to take in his probing tongue. Just the thought heated his blood. But it wasn't likely to happen. The lady was angry and it was his fault that she was.

He swallowed against the dryness in his throat. "I'm going to explain," he said, trying to keep his eyes on her face and off the rise and fall of her breasts beneath the buttons on her uniform. "That story was printed in error. I wrote it in a fit of anger, but I fully intended to edit it before it went to press—"

"Edit it? So you could add a few more barbs and innuendoes, a few more digs at Wallace or me or the hospital?"

Ted felt the faint throbbing in his right temple that signaled the start of a headache. He hadn't had many of them in his lifetime, but the few he'd suffered he could attribute to the infuriating woman in front of him. "Kyla, I'm trying to tell you that story was printed by mistake—"

"Yeah, and I'm a brain surgeon! Well, you've had the last laugh, Spencer. I admit defeat. Never let it be said that Kyla Bradford can dish it out but she can't take it. Now, let me go." She twisted away from him and fled down the corridor. At that moment she wanted to be far away from him, far away from the hospital.

Ted hurried after her and spun her around. "Look, my head's in a noose over this, as well. My editor's furious. He's threatening to lynch me at noon tomorrow unless I produce a follow-up that makes this place look so good people will want to check in for the weekend."

"That's your problem, Spencer."

"*Our* problem. I need your help—yours and Osgood's—if I'm going to make it a convincing follow-up."

Kyla's eyes raked over his face. What did he want from her? He'd come into her life, turning it upside down from the first night with his intriguing smile and his desirable body. Then he'd sliced her up in his newspaper and tossed her to the wolves. Now he expected her to *help* him?

"Let me get this straight. You wrote the story but forgot to edit it. Your paper printed it. I got raked over the coals, given an unpaid, unscheduled three-day vacation and you want *me* to keep *you* from being hung tomorrow at noon? Spencer, you can tell your editor to find a tall tree. I'll bring the rope."

"Wait a minute." Ted stopped her. "What did you say?"

"I said I'll bring the rope. Goodbye, Spencer."

AS KYLA UNDID THE BUTTONS of her uniform, she thought of how pleasurable it would be to see Ted's neck stretched three feet. What was it about the man that made her want to do battle with him? She didn't know, but one thing she knew for certain—he brought out the worst in her. She'd better get him out of her life before she did something else foolhardy. One more trip to Wallace's office would undoubtedly get her fired.

She stripped off the white garment, letting it fall in a pool at her feet, followed by her half-slip. Her career, her position in the ER was important to her. Important? It was everything to her.

Nursing school hadn't been easy. A rheumatoid disease had very nearly forced her to quit more than once, but she'd managed to stay in school, missing classes only when the pain in her joints was most acute. Fortunately, with vigorous treatment, the disease went into remission. Her doctors said it could flare up at times when her body was most stressed, such as during pregnancy.

Kyla feared becoming incapacitated again. She'd hated those times when she'd been unable to get out of bed. So, she'd made the only decision that made sense. She would not have children. No big deal, she'd concluded. Motherhood was probably overrated anyway.

The ER was her life and Ted Spencer had nearly wrecked that life. She'd struggled so hard to get where she was. And her career, she realized, would be the substitute for the children she would never have.

Ransacking her closet, she found a pair of beige cords and a red plaid shirt and quickly dressed. Might as well make the most of this enforced vacation, she thought, sliding her feet into a pair of brown loafers. There was nothing to be gained by sitting around feeling sorry for herself.

She knew very soon word of her suspension would filter through the hospital grapevine. She knew her friends would stick by her, but there would also be a few who'd feel she'd gotten what she deserved.

And perhaps she had.

Which faction would Roger be in? He'd been plenty hot about her disrupting his Operating Room.

And Spencer? Had it warmed his black heart that she'd received her just desserts?

She hadn't meant to tell him about the suspension. In the heat of the moment it had just slipped out. But he hadn't gloated at her admission. He'd looked stunned instead, and that puzzled her. Had their roles been reversed she would have gloried at his misery.

Kyla grabbed a sweater and tied the sleeves around her neck. A nature walk through Loose Park seemed the best prescription for forgetting the worst day of her life. Snatching up her keys, she stuffed them into the pocket of her cords and headed for the park.

She liked to walk, a repetitive act requiring no thought. The cadence of her feet on the sidewalk had a calming effect. The crunch of leaves beneath her feet and the pungent autumn air triggered pleasant memories of happier times. Football games. Hayrack rides. Helping her father make apple cider.

She paused at the curb to allow a car to pass before crossing the street to the park. Instead of passing, the car squealed to a lurching stop.

"Kyla!"

It was the second time today she'd heard that voice. She stood rooted to the spot, hoping Ted Spencer would drive on, but knowing there was slim chance of that happening.

"Kyla, I was on my way to your place. We've got to talk."

"I think we've said all we have to say to each other," she retorted, her voice raising a few decibels in spite of the fact she was trying to keep a tight rein on her emotions. "And how did you know where I live?"

"Ah! A reporter never reveals his sources." He threw her a raffish smile, then patted the empty seat beside him. "Hop in."

Kyla wouldn't even dignify his invitation with a reply. The sooner this man was out of her life the better. She turned away from him, crossed the street and walked in the direction of the duck pond.

Ted watched her leave, then pounded his fist against the steering wheel. Kyla was slowly driving him mad. She'd played him for a fool twice, and probably would again, given half a chance.

What was it about her? The way her eyes sparked when she was angry? The proud, defiant jut of her chin beneath that incredible pouting mouth? If he could tame this sassy Florence Nightingale, what would he find beneath the surface? Probably fire...passion...like nothing he'd ever known before. He slammed his gearshift into park and took off after her.

He found her kneeling at the edge of the pond, trying to coax a duck closer. The creature skimmed near, eyeballing first Kyla, then him.

"Here, try these."

Kyla started at the sound of his voice. He withdrew a crumpled bag of something from the pocket of his jacket and shook a few crumbling bits into her open hand.

"Barbecued potato chips? Are you trying to give him indigestion?"

"Trust me. He'll love 'em."

Ted dropped to his knees beside her. He caught a woodsy whiff of her that reminded him of soft pine needles. Her hair was loose, hanging to her shoulders, the late afternoon sun backlighting it so that it shimmered like fire around her face. He resisted the urge to touch it, to wind one silken curl around his finger.

"He probably will love 'em, but that doesn't mean this stuff is good for him."

"Yeah, well, some of us don't want to settle for what's good for us," he said, eyeing her lips with undisguised desire.

Kyla felt a sudden tingle travel up the curve of her spine with the speed of lightning. Quickly she glanced away, tossing a chip to the duck circling in front of her. His head dipped for the treat, then raised with a shake as he swallowed it.

Ted's gaze remained fastened on her. She could feel it trailing slowly and thoroughly over her, a sensation that made goose bumps dimple her skin. Without even touching her, he made her feel as if he had. Kyla fought for control of her suddenly erratic breathing.

His proximity was unsettling, overpowering. She got to her feet and walked toward the other side of the pond, feeling the need to put distance between them immediately. Ted seemed to have the power to disarm her, a feeling she didn't like. His presence was an unpleasant reminder of her fall from grace earlier today, the sad fact she'd come here to try to forget.

Ted tossed a few chips to the duck, then sauntered over toward Kyla, taking a seat beside her on the leaf-strewn knoll overlooking the pond.

"Don't you have something better to do, Spencer? Maybe another rotten story to write?"

A frown furrowed Ted's forehead. "I came by to say I'm sorry about your suspension. I . . . I didn't know."

Kyla shot him a cursory glance. His voice was low-pitched, a slow cadence near her ear, the sound of sincerity in it throwing her completely off guard. It also had a disturbing effect on her pulse rate.

"After you ran off I tried to square things for you with Osgood," he continued, "but he seems adamant about hanging your hide out to dry over this."

He was sitting too close for comfort. She knew she should get up and walk away. Now. While her traitorous body could still move. "I don't need you to remind me of the situation I'm in. I'm well aware of it. And of yours. Believe me, Spencer, I hope your editor does string you up tomorrow. Swinging from a tree is no more than you deserve."

Ted shrugged his broad shoulders. "I've been in tough spots before."

"I'll just bet you have. Now, would you please go. You've caused me enough grief for one day." She clamped her jaw and looked away from him. She wanted him to leave her alone, to walk out of her life as quickly as he'd walked into it. Since the night she'd met him, she hadn't drawn a peaceful breath. Even in her sleep he'd tormented her.

He reached out and turned her head back, cupping her upturned chin firmly between his thumb and forefinger. "Why are you being so damned pigheaded? Can't you at least listen to my explanation?"

"Talk is cheap, Spencer. Besides, what could you possibly say that would change anything?"

"You won't know unless you listen."

His thumb was slowly tracing the outline of her jaw. Once again his gaze settled on her mouth. Although his face was a good six inches away from hers, Kyla could almost feel the rough brush of his kiss. She moistened her lower lip. "Okay, pal, you've got two minutes."

He lowered his hand from her face and picked up a leaf, studying it for a moment. "That article was not an act of revenge against you. I wrote it, but I never intended it to be published. Accidentally, it was."

Ted crushed the leaf in his clenched fist. Kyla could feel the tension coming from him.

"I was feeling rotten from the afternoon. Dizzy. I went home without doing the rewrite."

Kyla couldn't have felt more stunned if someone had thrown a bucket of water at her. Dizzy. He'd been dizzy because of that stupid stunt she'd pulled in surgery yesterday. She was as much to blame for what had happened as he was!

She also knew what it was costing him in pride to admit to the unmacho weakness—at least, what he would consider a weakness—of vertigo.

"Anyway, I just came by to say I'm sorry, that's all."

She looked up at him. One dark curl rioted across his forehead. His eyes flickering over her were as earnest as a choirboy's. Well, maybe not that innocent, she decided on second thought.

"I...I think there should be some shared blame here, Spencer," she said, then extended her hand to him. "What do you say we declare a truce?"

Ted hesitated for a moment. "No more of your harebrained pranks?"

"As long as there are no more of your little forays into my Emergency Room for a hot story."

He flashed her a grin that showed a total lack of remorse.

Kyla eyed him warily. "That's the deal, Spencer. Take it or leave it."

Ted watched her gray eyes glitter beneath her lowered lashes. She looked like a wood nymph against the backdrop of the park's autumn colors. He wanted to kiss her, press her soft body to his, inhale her woodsy scent, taste her fiery lips, feel her hot desire spread through him.

"I'm waiting, Spencer."

He had to shake himself. "Yeah, deal," he said, but he didn't take her hand. Instead he reached for her, his arms sliding around her shoulders. He lowered his head, seeking the passion he knew was waiting for him.

He heard only her tiny gasp before his mouth closed over hers. Delicious. Her lips tasted as sweet as he'd expected them to. Soft. Like finespun silk, he thought as he deepened the kiss. Slowly he lowered her onto the bed of golden leaves beneath them.

It occurred to Kyla to resist, but only briefly. As his mouth moved on hers she felt warm shudders of desire tugging at her, wrapping her closer to him. She slipped into the circle of his arms and felt them tighten around her.

His lips were firm, his kiss slightly rough as she'd imagined it would be. The rough texture of his unshaven face rubbed against the smooth surface of her skin. As her lips parted to accept the thrust of his tongue, she heard a low moan tear from his throat. The masculine heat of him surrounded her, filling her nostrils with his special scent.

When he released her, she was breathless and she knew she'd been kissed—soundly and completely. "You shouldn't have done that," she said, trying to keep the huskiness out of her voice.

"Oh yes, I should have. I should have done that the first night I met you. And I intend to do it again soon— very soon."

The wind had changed directions. It was out of the north and definitely chillier, stirring up the leaves around them. But that wasn't the reason Kyla shivered. Ted would make good on his promise, and she wasn't sure she wanted to stop him.

She stood up, brushing the leaves from her clothes. Ted helped her, combing a few from her hair. He stole one last kiss from her before sprinting off. Kyla watched him go, feeling a strange aching need she feared only Ted Spencer could satisfy.

4

THAT EVENING KYLA CURLED UP on the sofa with a book she'd been trying to find time to read, determined to put all thoughts of Ted Spencer out of her mind. But after reading the same page four times, she realized she was not having much success banishing him from her thoughts. Pleasant images of him kept surfacing. His laugh, his smile, the feel of his lips, lustful and demanding, against hers.

"Enough!" she proclaimed and tossed the book aside. She stood up and paced the small living room, determined to forget this afternoon.

But even if she could push thoughts of him away, her body still recalled each separate sensation she'd experienced with startling clarity. Heat. Trembling. Desire. Never before had she slid so naturally into a man's arms, never before had she succumbed to a kiss so willingly.

Kyla sighed.

The balance of her evening loomed before her in unwanted hours. A light steady rain had begun to fall, its drizzle making lazy rivulets on the windowpane. She could hear its hushed patter on the wet leaves beneath the window.

One of autumn's sounds.

Like the crunch of leaves beneath them this afternoon as Ted . . .

Why did her thoughts continually return to him? Ted Spencer should be nothing more than an unpleasant memory, not someone she had to remind herself to forget.

Just then the phone rang and Kyla welcomed the diversion.

Before she could even get out a strained hello, Roger's voice barked across the wire. "Kyla, get yourself down here. The ER is a madhouse. We need all the help we can get."

"What's going on?" She heard the urgency in his voice.

"A semi carrying a load of hogs overturned on the interstate. The damned crazed porkers bolted, causing multicar pileups all over the downtown area. You'd think we were the only hospital in town, the way the injured are pouring in here."

"I'll throw on a uniform and be right over." She brushed away all thoughts of her suspension. This was an emergency—it took priority.

"Better take the side streets. The interstate's a snarl," Roger advised before she could hang up. "And drive carefully. Those ham hocks are everywhere. It'll take a month to round them all up."

TED WAS AT THE PAPER working on the hospital article follow-up when the call came in. Multicar accidents on I-70 near the downtown loop. It had to be more interesting than his rewrite! He snatched his jacket off the back of his chair and sprinted to the parking lot.

The rainslicked freeway was chaos when he reached the scene. All this caused by one overloaded semi full of hogs, he thought, surveying the devastation. For years Kansas City had fought to dispel its undignified image of an overgrown cow town. A truckload of pigs spilled out all over the city's downtown streets didn't exactly spell sophistication to the rest of the world. He winced at the thought of the national wire services picking up the story.

The flashing red lights of police cars were everywhere. The screaming siren of an ambulance pierced the night air as it roared away toward the hospital.

"Hey, Spence."

Ted heard his name being called in the silence following the ambulance's departure. Looking up he saw his friend on the police force, Frank Morton. He'd met Mort while covering a series of convenience store robberies a few years back.

"Over here, Spence," Mort shouted. "There's not an ambulance to spare and I've got a guy with a bad gash in his leg, bleeding like a stuck . . . um . . . hog. No pun intended," he said, glancing balefully at the unfortunate animal that had run in front of the victim's car.

The injured man lay pale and still on the grassy embankment beside the roadway, moaning softly. Ted took in the situation at a glance. He reached into Mort's first-aid kid for compresses and applied a steady pressure to the man's wound, fighting the revulsion he felt at the sight of the spurting blood. The same lightheadedness that had attacked him the day before in the surgery observation room threatened him now, but he supplanted it with action. "He needs a tourniquet, Mort," he said with false calmness.

Mort fumbled in the kit and produced one, then helped Ted apply it. "Where *are* those ambulances?" Mort searched around impatiently for one of the much-needed vehicles.

"We can't wait," Ted replied. "Let's get him into the back seat of your squad car. I'll work the tourniquet while you drive. Woodland . . . it's closest."

At the hospital Mort slid out of the front seat and snatched up a lone wheelchair he found in the entrance. Their patient let out an escalating groan as they transferred him into the chair.

"It's okay, buddy. Hang on just a minute or two more," Ted encouraged. Quickly he wheeled him inside, leaving Mort to move the police car.

As he whisked his charge through the doors of the ER, Ted caught himself searching the corridor for Kyla's tantalizing willowy frame before remembering that she wouldn't be there. The reason for her absence still weighed heavily on his conscience.

He hoped Osgood wasn't around at this late hour. The administrator considered him *persona non grata* around here and would no doubt personally deposit him on the sidewalk outside the building if he spotted him.

But instead of Osgood, his attention was caught by an unfamiliar stocky nurse who looked as if she could fill in as a longshoreman on her day off. She demanded an explanation for their presence, all the while scrutinizing Ted's remedial treatment with her practical eye.

A look of uneasiness clouded his features. He knew he was a bit rusty. It had been years since he'd reviewed a first-aid book—not since he was a Boy Scout.

"How long's this tourniquet been on?" she questioned, her large capable hands checking the victim's pulse.

"About ten minutes."

With a grumble, she acknowledged the information and spirited her patient away to the nearest unoccupied treatment room, leaving Ted staring after them.

As he turned to look for Mort to drive him back to the scene of the accident, he saw Kyla striding up the ER corridor between a fleet of gurneys and wheelchairs that lined the hallway. She looked so infuriatingly beautiful with her fiery hair piled atop her head, her white uniform doing little to camouflage the gentle curves of her hips and her narrow waist.

What was she doing here? Had Osgood reconsidered her suspension, after all?

Kyla looked up at that moment, her breath catching in her throat. What was Ted doing here? It didn't take too much imagination for her to guess. He had promised to stay out of her Emergency Room. Obviously his word meant nothing.

"Out ambulance chasing, Spencer?" she asked, marching toward him. Patients were crowding every corner of the ER. The last thing she needed was the press hanging around—especially this member of the press.

"You know, Kyla, someone really ought to teach you some manners." His voice carried a ring that bordered on annoyance.

She brought her hands to her hips and met his cool gaze. "And I suppose you think you're just the one to do it."

His green eyes appraised her slowly as if weighing up the prospect. The edges of his mouth curled into a hint of a smile. "It might be tempting to try."

Kyla longed to put him properly in his place, but Roger was waiting for a suture tray in Room Three and she still had a patient in X-ray. Still, she hated to leave, letting Spencer think he'd gotten the last word. She opened her mouth for one final barbed retort, but before she could deliver it she was interrupted by one of the other nurses.

"Mr. Spencer, that patient you brought in—"

"What about him?" Ted asked.

Kyla stared first at one and then the other in unconcealed surprise.

"His artery was severed. Your first aid just may have saved his life. He's on his way to surgery now. He should do fine. I just thought you might like to know."

"I'm glad to hear it." He said it quietly, obviously embarrassed by the praise.

Kyla wished she could amputate her tongue. How was she to know he'd been playing Good Samaritan instead of dastardly reporter? Somehow that excuse didn't make her feel any better about herself.

"Meg, would you mind taking a suture tray to Dr. Mason in Room Three for me?" Kyla asked the woman, with her eyes on Ted all the while.

When Meg had gone, Kyla cleared her throat nervously. "Well, it looks like I've just put my foot in my mouth."

Ted gave her a wry smile. "I'm certain that's nothing new for you."

"Look, Spencer, I'm not very good at apologies, so you'd better listen before I lose my nerve."

"Don't worry about it. You obviously have a pretty low opinion of me—"

"Opinions change."

He'd been about to turn and leave, but now he stopped and gave her an intense look. "Apology accepted," he said finally.

An awkward silence followed. Kyla stuffed her hands into her pockets. "I . . . uh . . . I've got to get busy, but I want to add my thanks to Meg's. Anyone who can earn her approval . . . well, you must be quite a guy."

"I've been trying to tell you that, lady," he said, slowly letting his mouth curl into a lazy grin.

"Yeah, well, don't let it go to your head, Spencer."

Before she could say any more, the ER doors slid open, admitting yet another freeway victim. The place was beginning to resemble a war zone.

THERE WAS LITTLE OPPORTUNITY the rest of the night to berate herself for her uncivil behavior toward Ted. The Emergency Room remained busy until four a.m.

"Go home, Kyla," Roger told her then. "We can take it from here. And thanks for coming in. You were a lifesaver."

"You don't have to tell me twice. I'm out of here." She grabbed her slicker and purse and headed for the ER door.

Ted stood on the opposite side. He'd been there for some time, observing the tension, the pace, the skill of Woodland's emergency team. That was the story he'd phoned into his paper—how one rugged little ER in the heart of the city handled a major crisis.

On a personal level he'd observed a lot more than that. He'd witnessed Kyla's tough gutsy exterior turn to tenderness and caring as she worked with the patients. What a strange mixture she was—a blend of both fire and ice, virtue and venom.

He wanted to know more about her. At least that was the reason he gave himself for being there waiting for her. "Can I tempt a certain lady with an offer of breakfast?" he asked when she came near enough. She looked radiant even though her shoulders sagged slightly from fatigue—a minor miracle, considering the night she'd put in.

Kyla smiled. After her poor manners earlier in the evening, she was surprised by his invitation. But he was asking, hands jammed into his pockets, a crooked smile playing at the corners of his mouth. He'd taken off his corduroy jacket and tied the sleeves around his waist. Now she knew why it always had that rumpled look.

"It's rather late," she hedged, not certain she had the strength left in her to deal with his tempting company. "And don't you have a story to write?"

"Already filed," he said. "And it's not late. It's only 1:30," he said, consulting his watch.

"It's 4:05," Kyla corrected.

"What!" He looked down at his watch again, then slid it off his arm and shook it a few times. "Damn cheap digital," he muttered. "So it's late. Have breakfast with me, anyway. An omelette and a cup of coffee will make a new woman of you *and* give you another chance to observe what a terrific guy I am."

Kyla laughed. "All right. You talked me into it. But on one condition—that you let me buy."

Ted frowned.

"A peace offering—for misjudging you earlier in the evening."

"Not necessary," he said, propelling her toward the exit to the parking lot.

"Yes, it is." Her eyes locked with his, and Kyla felt them absorb her.

"Okay then, but you may be sorry. I have a big appetite."

She may be sorry, Kyla thought, but it wouldn't be about picking up the check. If she wasn't careful she could find herself falling for this guy in a big way. She wasn't at all sure she had the time for a man in her life, and even if she did, she wasn't at all sure that man should be Ted.

The rain had stopped. Under the parking lot lights the pavement glistened with an iridescent oily hue. Ted opened the passenger door of the Porsche and Kyla slid in.

"Was this a game show prize, Spencer?" she asked, as he climbed in. It didn't fit—a man who wore a cheap digital did not drive a Porsche. She ran a hand respectfully across the smooth leather of the seat.

"What? Oh, the car." He backed out of the parking stall and onto the nearly deserted street. "A little family money," he said in a less than enlightening tone.

That was it? she thought. No explanation. "Perhaps there'll be enough left of that money to buy a new watch then. A Piaget or a Rolex, perhaps."

He laughed. "I guess I am a contradiction, aren't I?"

He was more of a contradiction than he realized, Kyla thought. And she didn't mean just the watch and the car. One minute he was a man she was prepared to dislike at first sight, the next he was someone she wanted to . . . *Dangerous thinking, Bradford,* she told herself. "You certainly keep a girl guessing."

"Don't mean to. Let's just say my family has money, but with the exception of the car—my one weakness— I prefer to make it on my own."

"Sounds commendable," she answered.

Ted didn't know how commendable it was. He'd never approved of his father's wealth or his ruthless business tactics. But now was not the time to think about that.

They'd reached the restaurant. Ted led her to a corner booth where they wouldn't be disturbed. He wanted her all to himself for as long as he could have her.

And he was determined that before the night was over, he'd taste the sweetness of those tempting full lips again, feel the lushness of her rounded breasts pushing against his chest.

"Your menu, Spencer." Kyla handed him the large sheet of laminated plastic.

"Huh? Oh. Thanks." He was really going to bowl her over with his charms if he kept this up, he told himself.

Damn! He was acting like a teenager on his first date. What had happened to all the smooth lines that had tripped so easily over his tongue in the past?

But he knew the answer to that.

This woman wouldn't be fooled by lines, no matter how clever they were. She hadn't been fooled by his bit of chicanery that night in the ER and she wouldn't be fooled now.

Honesty. It was his only hope.

"What would you like to order?" he asked. "I recommend the Texas-size omelette. It's their specialty."

"Sounds great," she answered, "since I don't see *crow* listed here."

Ted smiled. She could laugh at herself. He liked that.

"Two omelettes," he said to the waiter who was placing water glasses in front of them. "And bring us lots of coffee."

The waiter scribbled their order on his pale-green pad, then disappeared toward the kitchen.

Kyla leaned back in the cushioned seat and tried to relax. They were sitting side by side in the narrow booth. She would have felt safer across from him, she thought, forcing herself to ignore the feeling his nearness aroused.

To dispel her uncharacteristic tension she looked around the room. The all-night restaurant was a Kansas City tradition for after-hours diners and insomniacs. Its decor of soft lighting, green plaid carpeting and brass lanterns made it look cozy and intimate.

Too intimate.

She welcomed the clatter of pots and pans from the kitchen. It distracted her from Ted and the effect he was having on her.

"What were you doing on duty tonight?" Ted asked, his voice low and tantalizingly close to her ear. "I mean what about Osgood, your suspension . . ."

Kyla drew a shaky breath before finding her voice. "My suspension is still very much in force. And when Wallace finds out I was there helping out, he may very well make it permanent," she said. "But tonight my first concern was the ER, not Wallace or his disciplinary action."

Ted smiled. "I thought it might be something like that. I wouldn't worry about Osgood, though, if I were you. I think when he knows the facts, he'll come around."

Kyla glanced up at him curiously. "You seem pretty sure of that."

Ted grinned, thinking of the story he'd phoned in. Yes, he was certain Osgood would approve of what he read in the morning *Courier*. "Just a hunch," he said.

The waiter was back, this time with the coffee carafe, and poured them each a cup. When he'd gone, Ted glanced over at Kyla.

"Tell me," he said, "why did you choose the ER? I mean . . . why not Surgery or . . . Pediatrics, for instance?"

Kyla cupped her hands around her coffee mug as if they suddenly needed the warmth.

Pediatrics.

There'd been an opening in Peds. And she loved children, but . . . well, she'd just thought it best to keep children at arm's length. There'd be enough in life to remind her she would never have any of her own, without facing the fact each day at work.

Instead she'd opted for Emergency. And she loved the department, it's demanding pace, its constant surprises.

"Why not the ER?" She turned the question around with a philosophical shrug of her shoulders. "It suits me, don't you think?"

Ted's eyes were on her face. "It definitely suits you," he answered. "The action, the challenges, the unpredictability." He trailed one finger along the curve of her cheekbone, then across the fullness of her lower lip. "Definitely the unpredictability."

Kyla was acutely aware of the path his caress took. His fiery touch was like a brand. Her lower lip pulsed wildly beneath the roughened pad of his finger. She wanted him to kiss her. Again. She wanted to know if the experience was really as pleasurable as she remembered.

What was she doing? Fantasizing about a man she couldn't get along with for two minutes?

She pulled away.

They were like a pair of cats in a sack.

They clashed.

And Kyla wasn't sure why.

Just then the waiter was back, sliding large steaming platters in front of them. The aroma was ambrosia and Kyla realized how hungry she was after her busy night in the ER.

"So tell me, what do you do for fun? Besides way-laying reporters, that is?" Ted asked, diving into his omelette with gusto.

Kyla looked up and laughed, a bite poised on her fork. "I don't waylay reporters, unless, of course, they deserve it. And in your case, you did."

Ted nearly choked on a swallow of coffee. "That's your opinion. I say I was sabotaged. And you enjoyed every minute of it. Don't deny it."

"I did," she admitted frankly. Almost as much as she was enjoying his company now. Surprised at that realization, Kyla looked away and busied herself with her plate.

The conversation drifted to more casual topics and Kyla was relieved. They talked about everything and nothing, but every word brought them closer to understanding each other. Kyla learned he loved mountain streams, crossword puzzles and reading mysteries. In turn, she admitted her love of baseball, Chinese food and books that made her cry. They found they both had a passion for old movies and hated shopping for groceries.

She was glad she'd agreed to have breakfast with him. She was getting a totally different picture of Ted, one that she wanted to sort out at leisure, when she had the time to focus her mind on the many deep and varied facets of his personality.

When the waiter reappeared at their table with fresh coffee, Kyla refused the refill. She'd had three cups already—way past her limit and it was late, very late. "I have to try to sleep when I get home," she told Ted. "And speaking of sleep, I should be going. The sun's nearly up."

She reached for the check, remembering her promise to buy breakfast, but Ted was too fast for her. He snatched it up and headed for the cashier.

Kyla gathered up her belongings and followed him. "Ted Spencer, you are not a man of your word."

"I'll let you pay next time," he teased.

Next time? She wanted a next time, she realized. She wanted that very much.

When he dropped her at her car in the hospital parking lot, the sun was only a faint streak of pink in the sky bathing the contours of his face in its soft light. He had a beautiful smile. It tilted up crazily at the edges of his mouth, one corner higher than the other. Slightly awry, like his offbeat brand of humor. But his smile, like his humor, was very much a part of this man. Without thinking, Kyla reached up and touched one tilting corner of his mouth.

Her gesture unleashed in Ted all that he'd been holding back, all that he'd wanted to do all night. He captured her hand in his and laced his fingers through hers, feeling their heat. He bent his head to hers . . . slowly.

She moistened her lower lip, whether in anticipation or trepidation he wasn't sure.

Her breath was fire against his mouth.

Her fresh scent was driving him mad. He wanted this woman, like he'd never wanted a woman before.

She didn't pull away. Her lips were soft and tangy, the slight taste of coffee still lingering on them. He heard her soft sigh in the early morning stillness as he drew her body to his.

Kyla felt herself melt into his embrace. His chest was rock hard, and the softness of her breasts yielded against it. She wrapped her arms around his neck, her fingers finding their way into his hair's springy curls, tangling in them.

Her lips parted as if they had a mind of their own and his tongue dueled softly with hers. Desire swirled and rushed at her, demanding and frightening in its intensity, causing a sweet ache deep within her.

She heard a low groan tear from his throat as, hungrily, he deepened the kiss. His hands were splayed across her back. She could feel the passion in them as they slid over her. Her thoughts were chaotic. Her body screamed out for his touch.

As if he sensed that, Ted slid his hand over the fullness of one straining breast. His thumb brushed her nipple until it tautened beneath his touch. His other hand slid to her waist, then lower, drawing her closer to him until she could feel his hardness throbbing against her.

This was all happening too fast, she thought with the one small portion of her brain that was still function-

ing with some rationality. They had only recently de-
clared a truce, a shaky truce at that. Remembering, she
pulled away.

"Ted, it's very late. I should go." She reached for the
door handle of her Mustang. She wasn't in control
around him. He made her want more—more of him,
his kisses, his touch. Perhaps it was her ER training, but
she liked to be in control of any situation. And in this
one, she clearly was not.

Ted caught her hand on the door handle, pinning it
beneath his. Around them the dawn was quickly becoming morning. One by one the parking lot lights
were snapping off on their timers. The intrepid Kyla
Bradford was afraid, he thought. Of what? Of him?

But this was not the time or the place to go into it.
They had patched up their differences tonight. They
were off to a new start. It would be enough for now.
Time and the undeniable passion that was alive between them would take care of the rest.

"Good night, Kyla Bradford," he said.

She liked the way her name rolled off his tongue. It
was all hard consonants, yet he managed to make them
sound musical.

"Good night," she answered, trying to hide the
breathlessness in her voice. His kisses, the responses
he'd evoked in her had left her far shakier than she
wanted to admit.

"I'll see you home."

"Ted, that's not necessary. I'll be fine." She wanted to leave him now. At her door she might change her mind.

"I want to see that you get there safely. Nothing more." He brushed one final kiss across her swollen lips and turned to get into his car.

5

KYLA PULLED INTO THE DRIVE in front of the carriage house and glanced into her rearview mirror. She caught Ted's wave before he sped away into the light morning haze. She leaned back in her seat and sighed. Fatigue was quickly claiming her, the fatigue she hadn't felt while in Ted's company.

She'd enjoyed herself, she realized as she got out of the car. Seeing her home had not been necessary. Still, it had been a surprisingly thoughtful gesture. She had the feeling he was a man who treated his women with a mixture of gentleness and gallantry.

His women. The thought stopped her. What about the women in his life? He was thirty-five years old. He must have had several romantic involvements, maybe even a marriage. What did she really know about this man?

She found her morning edition of the *Courier* submerged in a puddle in front of her door. Her paperboy had terrific aim, she thought wryly, as she rescued the sodden mass. She carried it, dripping, inside, dropping it unceremoniously on the kitchen counter. She would have to dry it out in the microwave before she could even read it!

Ten minutes later she was out of her uniform and into her warm robe. She crawled into bed, carrying the paper with her. The microwave had shriveled it until the print was barely legible.

Ted's report of the overturned semi and the stampeding hogs occupied prime space on the front page along with a grim aerial photo of the pandemonium on the highway. Her eye stumbled over the misshapen print, reading as fast as the newspaper's desiccated condition would allow.

She admired his writing style. It was concise and factual. He'd added the right degree of emotion without the melodramatic overtones common to some journalists.

He'd given equal space to Woodland Memorial and the ER's expert care of the injured. Wallace would like that. She propped herself up higher on her bank of pillows and read on, duly impressed. With his clever flair for words, Ted had made the hospital and the night staff look good, damn good. He'd pulled it off, in one neat little package, the rewrite he'd needed to redeem himself in the administrator's eyes and save himself from his editor's lynching rope.

Last night he'd already come a long way toward redeeming himself in her eyes. Her mouth edged into a shameless smile. Bringing a finger to her lips, she traced their outline. A flush of warmth ran through her body as she recalled the sensations he'd aroused in her.

She'd discovered in him a gentleness that surprised her, a charm that delighted her . . . and a sexual chemistry that was so strong she wouldn't be able to deny it for too long. That thought frightened her. But she didn't want to think of the consequences right now. Besides, she'd never been one to worry about eventualities before—in anything. Maybe that's why she currently found herself in Wallace's disfavor.

Wallace would be pleased as Punch with Spencer now, but what about *her* position with the administrator? She had probably dug herself even deeper by ignoring her suspension and going into the ER last night. She'd only gone because they'd needed her help, but would Wallace see it that way?

No sense worrying about it now. She'd done what she'd done. Picking up the paper again, she decided to read until she got sleepy.

Turning to the inside page, her eye scanned the columns. There was an article about Leonard Daniels, Woodland's heart transplant patient, but it was not about his surgery. Instead, it was a powerful exposé about some of his recent business negotiations. A very damaging piece.

Who would write a story like that about a man who was still recovering from heart surgery? Her eyes flew to the byline.

Spencer!

Kyla couldn't believe what she'd read. She smoothed the paper out for easier reading and pored over the page. It was tough hard-nosed reporting.

Had Ted checked these facts?

True or not, he had come down hard on this guy.

She read through to the end, then tossed the paper aside. Jumbled thoughts rioted in her head. Was this the same man who had kissed her with such gentleness only moments before, who'd been concerned she get home safely? Just when she'd decided he wasn't a skunk, he began to show his stripe!

Kyla punched her pillow as if it were somehow responsible for this latest turn of events. She didn't want to believe it. Ted must have had some reason to write what he did. But what reason? And why attack Leonard Daniels when he was down? That was unforgivably ruthless.

She didn't want to think about it now. She'd been up all night. Now was not the time to try to consider possible explanations.

KYLA DIDN'T KNOW HOW LONG it had finally taken her to fall asleep, but when she awakened it was afternoon. She felt as though she were one of those unfortunate critters who had escaped the overturned semi last night and been made into bacon by the freeway traffic.

The phone rang and Kyla swore faintly. She'd forgotten to set her answering machine. Tossing off the covers, she hurried to the phone.

It was Wallace.

"Uh . . . Miss Bradford. It's you and not that infernal machine of yours."

She waited patiently while he complained about modern gadgetry, then finally got to the point of his call.

"In light of the latest hospital article in the *Courier* and, ah, um, in light of your unselfish work last night in the ER," he began in a long preamble, "I, um, I am reconsidering your suspension. You are to be reinstated, effective immediately."

Kyla was stunned into silence for a moment. She had never dreamed Wallace would do an about-face. She'd been certain he'd be furious, but instead he'd handed her a compliment of sorts, although he'd nearly strangled to death getting the words out.

"Thank you," she murmured, feeling relief surge through her as the full impact of it all began to hit her. Her job was important to her and her work record even more so. "What about my file? Will there be any mention of this on my record?"

"No, Miss Bradford," he replied, his voice taking on its more characteristically imperious tone. Kyla could almost see the scowl punctuating his comment. "Nothing in writing, but you can be certain it'll stay fresh in my mind for some time to come. I suggest that in the future you be on your best behavior."

This was the old Wallace she was used to. But she was pleased nonetheless. She was off the hook, her work record intact.

KYLA WAS HAPPY TO BE BACK in the ER. She hadn't heard from Ted in a few days, not since the night of the freeway melee. She was relieved. Her mind had been struggling to sort out the muddle of conflicting feelings that had her reeling.

Over the past few days she'd scanned the paper for his byline as if by reading his words she might discover the man he really was.

Subsequent articles about Leonard's Daniels did not appear, thereby giving her no clues to the reasons behind Ted's shockingly brutal report of a man for whom the city had nothing but the highest regard. She found only a few innocuous stories printed in the newspaper, but they revealed nothing salient about the man who'd written them.

Then, buried on the seventh page, Kyla discovered a very moving story carrying his byline. It concerned the street people, the city's homeless, and how they would fare in the upcoming winter weather. It was heartrending and touchingly anecdotal. She was surprised by the sensitivity in the writing, so very different from the abrasive article he'd written exposing Leonard Daniels.

Kyla was still puzzling over the difference as she sat sipping her coffee that night in the break room. She was thankful that the ER was quiet. They'd had only five patients so far. However, she was only three hours into her shift. Things could change at any moment. Friday night in Emergency could be bedlam, second only to the frantic activity of a Saturday night.

"Care if I join you?"

Kyla looked up to see Roger's lanky frame in the doorway. "Suit yourself." Generally she welcomed his company, but tonight she was in no mood for conversation. Instead, Ted and his confusing miscellany of articles occupied most of her thoughts.

Reading a man's writing was like looking through his closets, she thought. But she couldn't seem to identify Ted Spencer's true colors.

Roger ambled over to the battered couch, found a section that wasn't losing its stuffing and sat down. "I feel like the Maytag repairman tonight," he quipped.

"Don't knock it, Roger. It's either feast or famine around here, and I, for one, am going to enjoy the famine while it lasts."

"I'm not complaining," he said, as he unfolded his newspaper and quickly seemed to forget she was there.

A few minutes later, Allie sauntered in. Disinterestedly leafing through a dog-eared magazine, she alternated glances at it with conversation with Kyla about the deplorable menu they'd had lately in the hospital cafeteria. "We should send out for pizza," she lamented.

Kyla frowned at her. "Allie, I'm certain that's not on your diet." Allie was perpetually on a diet, but always managed to lose and gain the same number of pounds each week, making no dent in her pudgy figure.

Suddenly Roger's head appeared over the top of his paper like a well-oiled jack-in-the-box. "Kyla, that reporter you made short work of in surgery last week has another article in here about Daniels. I thought the last one was a hatchet job, but you should read this one."

"I'm sure Ted has a good reason for writing what he's writing," she said, jumping up from her chair. "After all, he's a responsible journalist—"

"You're on a first name basis with this guy?" Allie chimed in. "Last time I talked to you, you had a few choice names for him. Now, you're defending him?"

Kyla felt her face redden. Defending him? Was she? Yes, she was. Embarrassed and surprised at herself, she sat back down.

"Well, what are you looking at?" she snapped at Roger, who was grinning at her like a man who'd come unhinged.

"Now don't get testy, Kyla," he tittered, obviously enjoying his bit of fun. "Just because you've gone *ape* over this guy."

"I haven't gone *ape* over him," she said, but Roger wasn't listening. He was rolling off the couch over what he apparently thought was an amusing choice of words.

She looked to Allie for back-up, but her friend had joined in the merriment with Roger. "I thought I was working with a couple of professionals. Obviously, I'm not."

The last sight she had of them before she sailed out of the room was Roger holding his arms apelike, scratching his armpits.

THE NEXT NIGHT WAS HALLOWEEN, and Kyla was off duty. She'd prepared for the onslaught of tiny ghosts and goblins who were clever enough to discover that the carriage house hidden behind the gray stone mansion was inhabited. The steady stream of costumed figures seemed never-ending. She had to hand it to these kids. They were smarter than she expected. Either that, or each small troop was passing the word on to the next.

She groaned as she made what she hoped would be her final trip down the stairs to the front door with her nearly empty bag of treats. Why hadn't she turned out her lights!

There would have been no rest in the ER tonight, either, she consoled herself. Halloween usually brought with it a rash of minor injuries and a long procession of nervous mothers wanting to X-ray their children's jelly beans and chocolate bars.

This time, however, her nocturnal visitor was no small hairy monster or devil with a long stuffed tail. Her hand tightened around the sucker stick she was holding, snapping it in two.

Leaning against the doorjamb, resting his unmistakably adult frame against it, was an overgrown trick-or-treater. He wore a brown paper grocery sack over his head, with holes for eyes, and nose. She looked around for the child he most certainly had in tow, but saw none.

"Aren't you a little too old for this?" she asked sarcastically, stuffing a handful of suckers into the bag he held out to her. The guy should grow up!

"Too old? Never," he laughed, his words muffled through his mask. "No one's ever too old for Halloween."

Kyla was not amused.

"Aren't you going to invite me in?" he asked.

Suddenly she realized how vulnerable she was. The guy could be dangerous. Or crazy. Why else would he be out trick-or-treating at his age? She was all alone in her apartment, too far from the mansion to be heard if she screamed. She shoved at the door in an attempt to shut it, but one brown-loafered foot prevented it from closing.

"Halloween must have you spooked," he said, stripping off the grocery sack.

"Ted Spencer!" She exploded with an anger tinged with relief.

He stood framed in the doorway, grinning merrily. She tried hard not to notice that his tight jeans hugged him in all the right places and his tan sweater dipped to a vee in front, revealing a mat of dark sensuous chest hair.

"If you're not masquerading as a patient, you're masquerading as a . . . What are you supposed to be?"

He looked down at the hastily fashioned mask he held in his hands. "You don't like it?" he asked, putting it back on. The smile sneaking onto her lips told him she did.

"Hey, mister!" Ted whirled around to find a gang of costumed ten-year-olds advancing on him. "This is our territory. Find your own."

"Kyla, you gotta let me in," he pleaded as the pack closed in around him. Without waiting for permission he dodged past her, up the stairway, into the safety of her apartment.

He could hear Kyla below, appeasing the little ruffians with handfuls of candy, then shutting the door and climbing the stairs.

"Those people in the mansion out front sure give stingy Halloween candy," he said when she returned.

"Spencer, you didn't!"

A warm blush stained her cheeks, and her long hair fell to her shoulders in a luxuriant cascade of color that reminded him of russet leaves. "One miniature Tootsie Roll. Can you believe it?"

"I can't believe *you*." The man was certifiable. "I should throw you out and let that gang of kids make mincemeat out of you."

"Don't do that. I promise no tricks and I even brought the treats." He held out the bag she'd dropped the suckers into a few minutes earlier.

"I'm not interested in your Halloween candy," she announced, her hands on her hips.

She looked so inviting in her stretched-out gray sweatshirt and slim-fitting black jeans. Her feet were bare, her toenails painted an exotic coral shade that matched the blush on her cheeks.

"No, not candy." He shoved the bag at her.

Kyla accepted it reluctantly and peered inside. Underneath her donation of suckers were six white containers with wire handles. "Chinese food!"

Ted laughed, seeing the look of pure delight that lit up her face. He'd remembered it was her favorite and had picked it up at the last minute—in case he needed it for leverage.

"I'll get the plates," Kyla said, then disappeared into the kitchen. This man was moving into her life as swiftly as he'd dodged past her into her apartment to escape the pint-sized gang of evening marauders. And she was doing nothing to stop him.

This morning's paper had carried another article on Leonard Daniels. Roger had been right. The succeeding ones were getting even rougher, more damaging. Ted Spencer was obviously out for this man's blood. But why? She wanted to ask him about it, but not now.

No sense ruining a good Chinese dinner, she thought as the pungency of soy sauce tantalized her nostrils.

"There's a bottle of plum wine at the bottom." Ted suddenly appeared behind her. "Want some help with the cork?"

No sense ruining a good bottle of plum wine, either, she told herself. Yes, her questions could wait. "The corkscrew is in the drawer to the right of the stove."

Ted found it and went to work on the bottle. "I like your apartment," he said, nodding admiringly at the rich old woodwork. Her place had what his apartment lacked. Warmth. Homeyness. Perhaps it was the warm-hued wood or the touch of antiques that made it so inviting, but most probably it was the woman who lived in it. He thought of the home he'd grown up in as a child. Large, palatial, cold. So cold. This place wrapped its arms around him.

Kyla thought she saw a touch of melancholy in his face, but then the expression was gone, too fleeting for her to grasp. "Thanks. I did most of the restoration work myself."

"I'm impressed." He'd noticed the intricately carved ceiling moldings when he'd stepped into the living room. Now he saw they followed through to the kitchen, as well.

"Both the mansion and the carriage house are on the register of historical places. It's rumored that President Grover Cleveland once stabled his horse and carriage in what is now the garage below."

"Only rumored?" Ted asked, watching the way the warm glow of the overhead light accented her cheekbones and softened the color of her eyes to a pearl gray.

"There's no proof of it. One of the mansion's previous owners may have indulged in a bit of fancy to enhance the property's value."

The way he was looking at her was making her nervous. She set out the plates and napkins onto a serving tray. She added a couple of forks—just in case—since the restaurant had included chopsticks, obviously expecting their customers to dine in the traditional way. Carrying the tray into the living room she set it down on the low coffee table—Chinese food could not be eaten sitting at a kitchen table.

"Where are your wineglasses?" Ted called to her.

"I'll get them," she answered.

It was easier to find them herself than to try to explain their location. They had no doubt been shoved to the back of the cabinet. She'd done very little entertaining since she'd moved in. Even when she'd finished remodeling she hadn't thrown a party to celebrate. Furthermore, with her schedule in the ER, there was very little time for a social life.

Kyla moved the step stool into position and began her climb. Ted's eyes followed her ascent. Her soft slender body reeled slightly on the top step as she stretched to reach into the cabinet.

He should offer to help, he knew, but he was too busy enjoying the view.

The fabric of her jeans tightly hugged her derriere, causing his blood to heat and his palms to itch. Her long legs looked even longer as she stood on tiptoe to reach higher. The motion of it rocked the step stool, making it wobble beneath her.

"Be careful." Ted pitched forward to stabilize the short ladder with one foot on the bottom rung. He braced her slender bare ankle with one steadying hand, catching her swaying backside with the other.

"Maybe you'd better let me do that...before you fall and break something." He wasn't thinking of the glassware.

"Just steady this thing. I've got them."

She backed down the steps, the two tall flutes dangling from one hand. His palms slid up her sides as she descended, adding support she didn't really need, but which he'd been unable to resist giving. As her feet touched ground he pulled her into an embrace. "You could have fallen," he murmured.

Her face was flushed. He bent his head to kiss her lips that were just a breath away and noticed her eyes darken and grow solemn a moment before their mouths met. Her lips parted invitingly and his tongue sought her warmth within.

Their bodies melded together, softness meeting hardness. The glasses clinked behind him as her arms encircled his neck. His hands moved over her, tracing the outline of her ripe curves. Lush. Yielding.

She was making him forget the promise he'd made to himself, that he'd take this slow, let their relationship develop. Kyla was not a woman to take lightly. She was someone to fall in love with.

What was he thinking? The thought had an immediate cooling effect. He had to consider this carefully. He'd never been in love before and he wasn't sure he wanted to start now. If he did, however, this would be the woman. Of that he was certain.

He took a step back and looked down at her through a haze of desire. A slight smile teased at her lips. Yes, this would be the woman.

He cleared the knot that had lodged in his throat. "How about a glass of that wine before our food gets cold."

"Mmm. A good idea," she murmured and slid out of his arms. Her light woodsy scent wafted past him as she turned to the sink to rinse the glasses.

He helped her dry them with the soft cotton towel she'd tossed at him, then picked up the wine bottle and followed her into the living room.

They seated themselves on the floor in front of the low coffee table. "I'll do the honors," he said, picking up the bottle. He poured a splash of the plum wine into each flute, then handed one to Kyla and raised his in a toast. "To inauspicious beginnings. When a relationship begins as badly as ours, it can only get better."

Kyla laughed. They had gotten off to a bad start. But she'd hardly call their association a relationship at this point. What's more, she wasn't sure she wanted one, better or otherwise with this man.

His kiss had been warm, tender, exciting. She could still feel the heat of it on her lips, leaving her with the disconcerting feeling that she wanted more. Offering him an uncertain smile, she met his glass with the clink of crystal.

Taking a sip, she savored the flavor on her palate. "Mmm, good," she proclaimed. "And perfect with Chinese."

"Perfect." His eyes skimmed her face, her neck, until she felt the heat rise in her cheeks and her heartbeat accelerate.

She set her glass down on the coffee table in front of her a little harder than she'd intended. To busy her hands, she reached for a serving spoon, but Ted stopped her.

"Allow me. My treat, remember."

Ted was doing such a good job she left him to the task. He divided up the six containers, portioning out a sampling of each delicacy. Crab rangoon, pepper beef, cashew chicken. Each new item he heaped over steamed rice looked more appetizing than the last.

Sitting back she watched him work. He'd pushed the sleeves of his sweater up above his elbows, revealing tanned, muscled arms. He looked so appealing tonight—too appealing. His dark brown hair had been tossed by the gentle fall breezes and left tousled and unruly and so...touchable. She shoved the thought to the recesses of her mind as she picked up an egg roll and took a bite. "Mmm, shrimp. Spencer, this is heaven."

"If it isn't, it'll do until heaven comes along."

From the way he was looking at her, Kyla had the feeling he wasn't talking about the shrimp. His green eyes had darkened to a smoky shade and were studying her intently. She glanced away, afraid to fall under their spell, certain they had the power to capture a part of her she didn't want captured.

"More pepper beef?" she asked, picking up the carton and ladling another generous portion onto his plate. "It would be a shame to waste any of it."

"Are you trying to make me fat?"

"Fat? Spencer, have you ever seen a fat Chinese?"

"Now that you mention it . . ."

Then his eyes were on her again, this time on her lips, as if he were contemplating . . . she wasn't sure what.

"You have a crumb on your lips," he said. He reached out a hand, brushing it away with the tip of his index finger.

Kyla drew in a small ragged breath. Her heart missed a beat, then hammered wildly against her rib cage. A simple gesture, but strangely erotic and it unnerved her more than she cared to admit.

She had to speak to break the intensity of the moment. "I want to thank you, Spencer."

"For what? Brushing away a crumb?" His green eyes danced mischievously.

"No," she laughed, relieved by his banter. "I was referring to your piece in the paper the other day about the overturned semi."

"Oh, that." He tried a few bites of fried rice using chopsticks. "I never could get the hang of this."

"You made the ER look good. No, more than good . . . great. What I'm trying to say is that Wallace liked your comments—enough to rescind my suspension."

Ted paused in his attempt to spear a piece of cashew chicken with the end of one chopstick, and turned to look at her. "I'm glad," he said with a sincerity that touched her. "You belong in the ER. I saw that the other night. You really love it, don't you?"

Kyla shrugged her shoulders. She'd always found it difficult to talk about her deeper feelings—with anyone. The ER was important to her, but she'd always tried never to let it show how important.

Ted realized that a shrug was all the answer he was going to get from Kyla, but he hadn't really needed to ask. He'd seen her in action that night, seen her compassion *and* her vulnerability. Kyla not only loved the ER, she needed it.

He realized something else as well. If Kyla had seen that story, she'd also seen the one about Leonard Daniels. He was getting a lot of heat from those pieces, and he expected some from Kyla. He busied himself with his plate, continuing to stab at a morsel of chicken with one of his chopsticks.

"Why don't you use a fork?"

"A fork?" He shot her a pained look. "I'm striving for authenticity here, woman."

"I don't think that's how the Chinese do it. You're supposed to pick up your food with these, not practice some weird form of acupuncture on it. Here, let me show you." She took his hand, positioning the awkward utensils in it.

Ted sucked in a breath. Her light touch, her potent nearness nearly drove him wild. No woman had ever riddled him with such desire. Well once, but that had been many years ago, and he could hardly remember much about her now. But Kyla...

Perhaps he shouldn't have come here tonight.

He brushed the thought aside, and under her careful tutelage struggled to trap a large bite between the two slender sticks.

"There, you've got it," she announced. "Now, up to your mouth."

He tried to close the gap between the plate and his mouth as she directed, but halfway there the tidbit wobbled, then fell with a plunk onto his bed of rice.

"You dropped it, Spencer."

"I suppose you can do better?" he countered, knowing full well it would be out of character for her to resist a challenge.

"Observe the pro," she retorted, picking up the chopsticks and maneuvering them into position between her long tapered fingers.

She went after a strip of pepper beef with confidence. He watched with a wide grin on his face, waiting for her to fail, but she executed the move with perfect dexterity.

"That was just a fluke. You can't do it again."

"Says you, Spencer." Again her hand traveled from plate to mouth with oriental ease.

"I know when to concede defeat," he said with a laugh, raising his hands in mock surrender.

Kyla bestowed a small gloating smile on him and picked up her fork.

"A fork?" Ted's eyes widened questioningly.

"I don't want to spoil my perfect record," she explained with a wave of the conventional utensil.

"Kyla Bradford, you're a fraud."

Kyla's eyes narrowed. "I wouldn't talk about frauds if I were you, Spencer."

His answering laugh was a low rumble in his throat. He leaned closer and refilled her wineglass, one broad shoulder lightly brushing against her as he reached across. His musky scent pervaded her senses, making her more acutely aware of him than she wanted to be.

She took a deep steadying breath and lifted her glass. "Thank you for the dinner," she said, striving to lighten the mood the evening had drifted into. "If you hadn't come by, I'd probably have settled for a microwave pizza or something as equally dull."

"Then I'm glad I came to your rescue." He brushed her cheek with the backs of his fingers. "I hate to think of you eating alone. Doing anything alone."

Kyla shifted her position on the floor and looked away, the touch of his hand against her cheek seared into her memory. "Actually, I like time to myself. They say if you like yourself, you don't mind your own company. But eating is one thing I don't like to do alone."

"I can think of several others," he said, his innuendo heavy in the air between them.

A mental picture of Ted's long, lean body lying naked next to hers popped into her mind. She shook her head to dispel the image. She'd had too much wine, she was sure. Why else would her imagination play such X-rated tricks on her?

Ted took her glass and set it down next to his, then reached for her hand. He felt the moisture in her palm, the heat in her fingers and knew she was as affected by the evening as he was. She didn't resist, but allowed herself to be drawn into his arms. His lips found hers, moving against them with delicious ease. The lingering flavor of the wine on their fullness made them taste even sweeter.

His hands tangled in her hair, the silken strands cascading through his fingers, its clean fresh scent reminding him of a cool fall breeze. He traced the outline of her lips with his tongue, memorizing its shape, its texture. He heard her soft sigh, a whisper against his mouth. She was more delectable than his most erotic fantasy of her.

He pulled her soft yielding body closer and lowered her to the carpet. She felt wonderful beneath him, all curves and roundness. He was on fire, drunk on the essence of her.

His hand cupped one breast through the layer of her sweatshirt as he dropped a flood of tiny kisses along the curve of her cheek, her closed eyelids, her temple where a pulse beat wildly.

Kyla savored the exciting sensations that engulfed her—powerful sensations like she'd never experienced before. The wine and Ted's kisses were making her forget that she didn't really know him. He was making her forget that she had questions. If only he'd stop kissing her she could remember what they were.

But she didn't want him to stop. This felt so good, his hand sliding under her sweatshirt, caressing her breast, bare under her shirt, stroking, stroking toward the tip, his thumb rough as it flicked across its now hardened peak.

Her mind shut down all rationality. She could only feel, feel the magic in his hands, savor the taste of his mouth.

Questions. She'd had questions when Ted arrived. Again that vague thought tried to fight past the sensations that stormed her body.

They needed to talk. Clutching his shoulder she slid her mouth from his, then braced herself against him, increasing the distance between them. A safer distance for talking.

Ted allowed her to draw away. He leaned back on one elbow, studying her face in the soft light of the living room. She was unsure of him and he didn't blame her. He sat up and held out a hand.

Kyla took it and let him pull her up to a sitting position.

"More wine?" he asked. He was going to need it if she started asking questions about his recent write-up on Daniels.

Kyla shook her head. No more wine. She needed to be able to think straight.

Ted poured the remainder of the bottle into his glass and took a swallow. He might as well open the discussion. "You've seen my bylines . . ."

"Most of them." Her voice quivered.

Ted looked down at his glass and swirled the dark liquid around to avoid facing the accusatory look in her eyes. His exposé on Daniels was tough, and likely to get tougher before it was over. There were other men in the city who were going to feel his bite before he was through.

He took a deep breath and met her gaze headlong. He wanted her to understand. "Kyla, Leonard Daniels is a slumlord. He needs to be exposed—"

"The man just received a new heart, for heaven's sake." Her voice had lost its tremulousness.

"Yeah, well, I wish it would help. His old one certainly wasn't the most benevolent—"

"He's one of the city's most generous benefactors—"

"That's only to salve his guilty conscience. The guy makes a mint off the unfortunate in this city, then gives a tiny portion of that back and gets a tax write-off and a bronze plaque for it."

He realized his voice had raised. The campaign was important to him. He'd gone out on a limb, exposing one of the city's stalwart, but this was no popularity contest. He'd known that going in. What he did want, however, was Kyla's trust. And it wouldn't be easy to win. She didn't like reporters, he knew, and right now he must seem like a real ogre.

"Kyla, trust me, please. This is dirty business, I know, but it's the only way." Ted got to his feet, pacing the living room.

Kyla watched the play of emotions across his face. She wanted to trust him. She'd even defended him last night to Roger and Allie. But reporters, she knew, could be insensitive. Merkle and his pals being prime examples.

Trust him? Could she do that? She reminded herself of how he'd brazenly lied his way into her department, faking belly pain the night of Leonard Daniels's surgery. On the other hand, she had to admit that he'd never hung around the ER like Merkle and his ilk—before or since. And the night she'd accused him of being an ambulance chaser, he'd been performing a mission of mercy. She still remembered her embarrassment over that incident.

"Let's say I believe you. But what I don't understand is why now? I mean, why print this while Leonard's still recovering from surgery? Couldn't it have waited?"

Ted lowered his head and rubbed the back of his neck. It felt stiff and tight. "My timing may have been lousy, but I had to go with the piece when it broke. I'm a reporter, Kyla, and I won't apologize for it."

Kyla stood up and walked over to him, touching his cheek. "I'm sorry. I shouldn't have asked you that. If you considered the story important—necessary—well, I'm sure you know what you're doing."

Did he know what he was doing? He'd better damn well be sure, if he was asking Kyla to trust him. He didn't want to hurt her. Perhaps he'd been so all-fired anxious to get this guy that he'd been unnecessarily ruthless. Damn, but this woman had a way of confusing him.

He gave her an uncertain smile and a tender kiss, then moved away from her. He had to tell her good-night and get out of here before he was tempted to draw her into his arms again. He wanted to make love to her, but when he did, he didn't want any doubts about him to get in the way.

6

NOVEMBER BLEW IN on a balmy breeze. Kyla watched workmen string the Country Club Plaza Christmas lights, draping a myriad of bulbs over the buildings' Spanish-style towers and cupolas.

She was meeting her mother for an early lunch at a sidewalk café. Ruth Bradford was in town to do some shopping, and Kyla had suggested the restaurant knowing that very soon sliding glass doors would enclose the tables, protecting diners from Kansas City's chilly winter. For today, however, she could enjoy the weather as the breeze fluttered the pink linen tablecloth and the petals of the fall flowers in the bud vase in front of her.

While she waited for her mother, she sipped a glass of iced tea and thought about Spencer's crazy trick or treat caper the evening before. After he'd left she'd lain awake for hours, sorting through certain facts.

One, she had a tendency to act impulsively, she knew. Hadn't Wallace pointed out this impetuousness to her on more than one occasion? And he was right. For the most part, the habit hadn't proven to be such a bad one—except where Ted Spencer was concerned. Two, acting impulsively was a habit that could prove dangerous when it came to men—when it came to Spencer. Three, she needed to be more cautious when she was around him. Especially since she didn't understand why he affected her the way he did.

But the part that eluded her was what she should do about Fact Three. The only surefire way she knew of to exert the required caution was to avoid seeing him again.

And that was the decision she'd arrived at this morning.

In spite of this new resolve, Spencer continued to pop into her thoughts. Her mind seemed to conjure him up at odd moments—like now. She watched as a tall, rumpled-looking male figure paused on the sidewalk opposite the restaurant and spoke to the workers stringing the garlands of lights. He had the same wide shoulders, the same relaxed stance, and was followed by the same *photographer!*

She would recognize Blood Hound anywhere. There could not possibly be two crazy creatures like him in the world. He was capturing the work in progress with his camera, while Spencer conducted his casual sidewalk interview.

"Oh, what a wonderful choice of restaurants, Kyla." Kyla looked up to see her mother's smiling face. "You look strange, honey. Are you all right?"

"I'm fine, Mother." She gave a furtive glance across the street. "But actually the food's not that good here. I don't know why I suggested it. Let's go somewhere else." She started to rise from her chair but her mother sat down.

"Oh, no. Even if the food isn't that exciting, the atmosphere is lovely—like a Parisian café," she said, arranging her packages on the chair next to her. "After we order, I'll show you what I bought. Your father will love me in it."

Kyla gave in with a graceful smile.

Ruth Bradford was a delightful woman, tall and slender like her daughter, her auburn hair now generously streaked with silver. She was warm, loving and intensely concerned about her children's happiness. Her three sons were all happily married; Kyla was her one loose end.

Ruth's soft gray eyes surveyed Kyla carefully. "Are you sure you're all right, honey? You're not working too hard, I hope. I know you don't like talking about it, but I do worry about a recurrence of your arthritis."

Kyla swallowed hard. She didn't like talking about it or thinking about it, either. Her rheumatoid disease hadn't been a problem for years, but she knew her mother still worried. Kyla smiled reassuringly. "No, I'm not working too hard. I'm fine. Really."

Her mother gave her one last anxious look, then switched the subject to the latest news from home and the fall apple crop. Kyla tried to focus on the conversation, but it was difficult. She risked another glance across the street. Spencer was still there.

"What's captured your attention?" Ruth's eyes followed Kyla's gaze. "Oh, they're hanging the Christmas lights. How interesting."

Kyla looked quickly away, not wanting her mother to notice the subject of her surveillance. The waiter had taken their order and was now back with the food. "This looks delicious. I'm hungrier than I thought."

"Good," Ruth said. "You're looking entirely too thin."

"Mother, don't start in on that," Kyla said, a few lines of a frown pleating her forehead as she realized she was in for another of her mother's lectures about her eating habits.

"I just think a young lady who's taken courses on nutrition would realize the importance of a well-rounded diet instead of surviving on microwave pizza."

"I do occasionally eat other things, Mother." Kyla thought of last night's oriental feast. She could barely recall the taste of the food, but the flavor of Ted's kisses came to mind with clarity, as well as the longings he'd stirred in her. Her hand clenched around her glass of iced tea as she reminded herself of her decision to avoid seeing him again. She would have to remember to stock up on microwave pizzas.

"Oh, I almost forgot. I brought pictures of the new baby." Ruth fished in her purse for the snapshots. Kyla's older brother Tim and his wife Beth had had an eight-pound baby girl the week before—their third.

"Isn't she precious?" her mother asked as she spread out the color prints for Kyla to see.

Kyla had to admit she was. All soft and cuddly and pink. Something wrenched inside of her as she looked at the pictures.

"The christening is in two weeks and Tim and Beth want you to be Erin's godmother."

Kyla tried to smile, tried to be pleased by the honor. It was something she was going to have to get used to. She couldn't avoid children for the rest of her life. The world was full of them, and her brothers seemed capable of producing them in endless numbers.

"Tell Beth and Tim I'm happy for them and of course I'll be godmother for Erin if they want me," she said, as her mother gathered up the pictures and returned them to her purse.

When Ruth motioned to the waiter for a refill on her coffee, Kyla took the opportunity to risk another glance across the street. She sighed in relief. Spencer was gone! Now perhaps she could get him off her mind—at least for the afternoon. She finished her crabmeat salad and listened to her mother outlining the family's plans for Thanksgiving.

Then a sound caught her attention—an ominously familiar click-whir. Kyla looked up, straight into the big round eye of Blood Hound's camera. Click-whir. Click-whir.

Ted Spencer stood beside him, grinning broadly. "He just can't resist photographing lovely women," he said, charm oozing from every male pore.

"You two know each other?" Ruth asked, glancing hopefully from Ted to her daughter, then back again.

"Yes, Mother, we do." Kyla introduced first him, then Blood Hound, whose wild red hair looked even more bizarre than she'd remembered.

Ruth looked at the photographer carefully as if she were trying to identify what cartoon character he reminded her of. "Why don't you both join us," she said, moving her packages to make room.

Ted didn't hesitate. He slid his tall frame into the chair beside Kyla while Blood Hound fumbled with his camera equipment, finally seating himself on the other side.

Ted instantly bewitched her mother with his politeness and charm, and Kyla gave up any hope of shortening the lunch meeting and making a quick escape.

He seemed genuinely interested in hearing all about the day-to-day operation of the apple orchard as well as about Ruth Bradford's grandchildren. And Ruth Bradford seemed equally fascinated with him.

Kyla was more than willing to let the conversation sail along without her, but Ted wasn't. "I'm sure Blood Hound will be happy to give you and your mother copies of the pictures he took once they're developed," he said, his eyes smiling into hers. "Two Lovely Women Lunching At Café." He said it as if he were captioning it.

"Thank you," she replied. His muscle-hard thigh rested against her knee. She shifted her body away, but Ted shifted too, bringing them into contact again. She took a sip of iced tea and tried to relax.

The talk switched to Ted's assignment for today, a behind-the-scenes story of the hard work involved in turning the renowned shopping plaza into an enchanted wonderland of lights for the holidays, a Kansas City tradition for more than fifty years. This story, like the one about the homeless, would be vivid and warm and skillfully drawn, she knew. So different from his investigative piece on Leonard Daniels's activities.

"When I was first starting out I covered this sort of action all the time. I miss it," Ted added.

"Why are you doing it today?" Ruth asked.

Because it was just her luck, Kyla thought to herself, trying to avoid looking at Ted's broad hands and tapered fingers and remembering how they'd felt moving over her bare skin the night before.

"Everyone in Features is out with the flu, so they sent Blood Hound and me."

Ted smiled at Ruth, then turned his dancing green eyes on Kyla.

How could November be so warm? she wondered. "I'm anxious to read it. I know it will be a good story," she said with sincerity.

"Thank you." He took her hand, trailing his thumb slowly across the back of it, holding it a moment or two before releasing it.

Kyla noticed her mother watching discreetly from across the table. Ruth Bradford hadn't missed the hand-touching or the slightly awkward thank-yous being passed between them, Kyla was certain.

"Are you from Kansas City, Ted?" Her mother's question sounded innocuous enough on the surface, but Kyla knew differently. The woman would like nothing better than to see her happily married, and Ted Spencer had just become an unsuspecting candidate.

"I'm Kansas City born and bred, Mrs. B." Ted leaned forward, allowing her the full force of his charm.

Kyla couldn't listen.

Blood Hound, who had added very few comments throughout the conversation, now began to fidget, playing with the settings on his camera. He looked around for possible subjects—waiters, shoppers passing by.

She had to get out of here!

Her mother's laugh rippled across the table and Kyla caught her words. "Kyla was a beautiful child, with two long red braids and a face full of freckles." How had the conversation shifted from Spencer's place of birth to her childhood? And what had she missed in between?

Ted turned toward her, a smile twitching at his lips. "I don't see any freckles now. She must have outgrown them."

"Oh, she still has a few," her mother said.

She did have, as a matter of fact, but not in visible places. By the way he was looking at her, Kyla felt he suspected that and would enjoy searching for them. It made her blood tingle.

"Before you break out my baby pictures, Mother, I do have to leave." She stood up, shoving back her chair with more force than she'd intended. "I'm due at the hospital at two-thirty. And I believe you have more shopping to do."

Ruth consulted her watch. "How did it get so late?"

"That's my fault, Mrs. B. I'm afraid I monopolized your time."

She turned to Ted. "Oh, but I enjoyed it. I hope we meet again soon."

"I'm certain we will," he said, leaving Kyla with no doubt that meant it.

THAT PROVED TO BE the last weather-perfect day the city saw for a week. A bank of clouds had taken up residence and refused to move out, leaving the citizens of Kansas City digging out warmer clothes and rain gear.

When the rain finally stopped, the chilling dampness remained, permeating everyone's bones—which brought on a rash of colds and bronchial conditions. The ER was flooded with patients requiring treatment, particularly the elderly and the chronically ill.

Kyla and her team had been busy all evening. Her shift was over in ten minutes, but she had a stack of charts to sign off on before she could leave.

As she picked up the first one, an obscenity splintered the silence. Kyla raised her head with a start.

"What's that commotion?" She tossed down her pen and went to investigate. Allie followed, close on her heels.

The commotion was just coming through the Emergency Room doors as they got there. About two hundred pounds of strident voice and body odor, riding in a wheelchair—with Ted Spencer pushing him.

Jane, the admitting clerk, ran along behind, waving a blue sheet of paper at the crusty fellow. "You have to fill this out before you can be treated."

"I don't want to be treated or poked or thumped on, either. Dammit! I told you that, woman." He shook his fist at Jane.

Jane retreated a few steps and looked to Kyla for help.

"It's all right, Jane. The form can wait a little while."

"It can wait more than a little while," the man bellowed at Kyla. "Ted, take me back."

His roaring outburst brought on a fit of raucous coughing. Kyla glanced up at Ted. His face was serious, a worried frown marking his forehead.

Was this man a relative?

Kyla curbed her usual curiosity. There wasn't time to pursue the subject. Whatever the relationship between the two, the man needed attention.

Kyla's voice was calm and patient as she bent down to wheelchair level. "Sir, may I have your name?"

He narrowed his eyes and glowered back at her. "What for?"

"So I know what to call you."

"What do I call *you*?"

Kyla laughed. "That's a fair question. I'm Kyla Bradford." She smiled and extended her hand.

He ignored it, scowling at her. "Campy McDuff," he said finally. "But I don't want none of your medicine. I can take care of myself. Always have."

She looked up at Ted. Mutual concern was evident in the glance they exchanged.

"Kyla, I'm afraid Campy may have pneumonia. He's slept outside in the rain and the dampness for the past week."

Kyla's eyebrow raised in surprise. So this was one of the street people Ted had written about. She hadn't realized to what extent he involved himself with his subjects.

"I think you may be right. We'll get him into a treatment room and let the doctor examine him."

"No such thing! No such thing!" Campy yammered between bouts of coughing. "I'm getting out of here."

He was all strength and wild determination as he pushed on the arms of the wheelchair and ejected himself from his seat. His legs tottered under him.

Kyla and Allie acted quickly, steadying his ponderous bulk before he could fall, and with Ted's help returned him to the wheelchair. Campy's gamy odor was offensive, but at the moment his need for medical attention took precedence over his need for a bath.

"Ted, Mr. McDuff needs care, but before he can be treated, we must have his permission," Kyla said over the top of Campy's head.

"Don't talk about me like I ain't sittin' right here. And I ain't givin' nobody my permission. Ted, let's go. I feel just fine."

Ted exhaled slowly. "Campy, we've been all through this. You agreed to come here and let the doctor check you out."

"Hmmph! Don't remember it."

"Campy..." Ted's voice was laced with exasperation.

"Aw right, aw right. But just a look-see. I ain't takin' no medicine and I ain't gettin' no shot." His lower lip jutted out like that of a spoiled child.

Before he could change his mind, Kyla wheeled him into the nearest room. With Allie and Ted's assistance, and the bare minimum from Campy, they got him onto the examining table.

The small army worked to relieve him of his several layers of shirts, sized with months of grime and perspiration. In the middle of the tug-of-war Roger sauntered in and immediately recognized Ted. He skewered Kyla with a narrow look that told her she was skating on thin ice if this was more of her "monkey business." Before Kyla could respond, Campy demonstrated his reason for being there with an attack of coughing and Roger's expression changed to one of immediate concern.

As if fearing bodily injury from Roger's stethoscope, Campy's eyes widened in terror. Ted had to cajole him into allowing the doctor to listen to his chest.

Roger's examination took only minutes. "I'll need X-rays on him. Two views." He gave the order, then disappeared from the room, leaving Kyla to make the arrangements.

A short while later the X-rays confirmed Campy's pneumonia. "In his debilitated state we'll have to admit him," Roger announced.

Kyla groaned. "Do you want to tell him or shall I?"

"I'd sooner suture a two-year-old," he said, then ambled off, muttering something about a nurse's proficiency for diplomacy.

Kyla shot him an evil glance he didn't see, then screwed up her courage to face Campy McDuff with the news that he would have a new address for the next few days.

But the street person was not receptive. "I ain't staying in no hospital," he thundered when she told him. He ripped off the patient gown they'd managed to get him into earlier. "Get me my clothes, Ted. I'm goin' back to my casket before the others steal it right out from under me—if they ain't already done it."

Ted met Kyla's widened gray eyes. "Yes, casket," he said. "Campy's current place of residence is an old discarded casket behind a coffin works."

"A top-of-the-line casket," Campy tagged onto Ted's sentence, as if that qualifier raised his standard of living a few notches. "Now, are you gonna get me my clothes or am I gonna have to walk out of here naked as a jaybird?"

"Give me a minute or two with him," Ted said quietly.

Kyla nodded her assent, then left the pair alone, wondering who would come out the victor, and placing her bet on Campy McDuff. She picked up the chart Jane had hastily made up on him and jotted down a few notations.

Ted had filled out the information sheet, she noted, but he'd left blank the spaces for Address, Phone, Employer, Insurance. She chewed thoughtfully on the end of her pen, only then realizing the full import of Ted's article about the homeless. These people were real human beings even if they had a few blank spaces in their lives.

A daughter Louise was listed under Next of Kin, but with a question mark for her address. Once upon a time there'd been someone in Campy's life. He'd had a family, a past.

Her eyes skimmed to the bottom of the page where Ted had listed his own name under Person Responsible for Account. She stared at it, her mouth gaping.

"He doesn't like it, but he's agreed to stay," Ted murmured into her right ear, planted a kiss on her neck and then smiled at her startled reaction.

Caution, Kyla reminded herself, was a virtue she lacked. She remembered her vow to keep herself at a healthy distance from this man. But how did she do that?

The rough beginnings of a beard shadowed the lower half of his face, giving him an earthy appeal, an appeal she tried hard not to notice. She moved a step or two away from his distracting nearness. She was, after all, still on duty.

The night shift had arrived, but she had charts to complete, including Campy McDuff's. She tapped her pen against the form Ted had signed. "Don't you realize that with the high cost of medical care, you may have to hock your Porsche to pay this bill?"

Ted threaded his fingers through his hair. "Look, the guy saved my life once. I owe him."

Kyla realized how little she really knew about Ted. She also realized this was all he intended to say on the matter. Well, it was his business. She never should have broached the subject. "I'm glad you convinced him to stay. How did you manage that?"

"It wasn't easy. I had to promise him I'd keep an eye on that casket of his."

Kyla arched an eyebrow at him. "And how do you plan to do that? Sleep in it yourself?"

"Not on a bet," he answered, then smiled. "Don't worry. I'll think of something."

"I'm sure you will." A man who could convince Campy McDuff to stay in the hospital could do anything. With a final flourish of her pen, she signed off on the chart. "I'd better call Admitting and get him to his room before he changes his mind."

WHEN SHE FINALLY FINISHED UP in the ER, Kyla decided to look in on Campy. She told herself she merely wanted to be sure the nurses could handle the bundle of trouble she'd sent their way. But the truth was she couldn't seem to stay away from Ted. Besides, her curiosity was getting the better of her, despite the fact she'd told herself Ted's affairs were no concern of hers.

Discordant howls met her ears as soon as she stepped off the elevator. She followed the sounds to Campy's room. Two nursing aides were giving him a bath, with the vagrant protesting resoundingly.

Kyla backed out of the room, deciding it was best to wait in the hall until they had finished. She looked for Ted, then rationalized her disappointment that he was nowhere around. Why should he be? Campy was in good hands now. Perhaps she should just stop by the desk, offer her condolences to the staff and leave.

Just then the elevator doors opened, and Ted stepped off, a cup of coffee in his hand. His brown leather jacket molded itself perfectly across the width of his shoulders, tapering to the leanness of his waist, and his jeans hugged his lower body with only one word to describe it: *sensual*.

His eyes brightened when he saw her, his face losing the creases of fatigue she'd caught in it a moment before. He lifted his cup. "I'd have brought you some if I'd known you were here. Want to share?"

Kyla shook her head. No caffeine. She needed to sleep when she got home, but at the moment sleep was the last thing on her mind.

"I want to thank you for your help tonight," he said. "It was appreciated."

He stood close, too close. She could smell the coffee on his breath, see the pulse beat lightly on the left side of his neck. "No thanks are necessary. I was just doing my job."

"But you're off duty now, Florence Nightingale. Or is this part of your job? Checking on patients after they've been sent to the floor?" His tone was light, teasing.

Kyla felt the color rise in her cheeks. Before she could think of a comeback, the door to Campy's room flew open and the two aides staggered out, looking as if they deserved combat pay for their night's work. Campy's loud curse followed them. Ted and Kyla exchanged glances, then laughed.

"At least he's clean," Ted ventured. "Shall we go in?"

Campy McDuff looked like a different person without the layers of dirt. His silver-gray hair was scrubbed and neatly parted on the side. The crinkly hairs of his beard glistened with cleanliness. He rested against two plump white pillows, an oxygen cannula tilted into his nostrils.

"They said I needed a bath!" He wore an aggrieved expression.

"You did, you old reprobate." Ted gave him a quick jab on the arm, then motioned Kyla forward. "You have a visitor."

Campy's eyes flashed toward Kyla, then back to Ted. "I don't want nothin' to do with her. She said I had to stay here."

"That's right," she addressed him. "But it's for your own good."

"My own good! I know my own good and this ain't it. Ted, my casket—I just know Hanks or Freddie will steal it. It's the best digs around and it belongs to me."

"I know, I know. I said I'd keep an eye on things and I will," Ted promised. He looked at Kyla and winked.

She smiled back, feeling the magic of the unlikely friendship between the two men.

"Then get out of here and see to it," Campy said, waving his arm in a shooing action. "And take her with you."

Ted gave him a warning scowl. "Okay, we'll leave, but only if you promise to behave yourself."

Campy pursed his lips into a pout.

"Campy...?"

"Okay, okay, I will. Now git."

Ted led Kyla out of the room. "I have a promise to keep," he said, closing the old fellow's door behind him. "Care to come along?"

She knew she should give some excuse and go home. Now. She also knew she wouldn't. She had to know more about this man and his curious relationship with Campy McDuff. Spencer was a bundle of contradictions. And to Kyla, contradictions were a challenge.

"I'm too keyed up to go home and try to sleep."

He guided her toward the parking lot, one arm around her waist. She could smell the rich leather of his jacket mingled with that disarming scent of his that reminded her he was all male. Her senses reeled.

"How did you become involved with Campy?" she asked. Talk. Talk would keep her from thinking about the man beside her.

"I met the old maverick a couple of years back while I was doing a feature on the homeless."

"Campy let you interview him?"

Ted laughed. "No, hardly. These people aren't about to talk to just anyone. They don't have a lot of trust. Most of them have been hurt by life, by people. And I wasn't really after an interview. I wanted to know how they survived from day to day, what problems they encountered, what had put them there in the first place. So I went on the street as one of them. I knew it was the only way they were going to open up to me, to trust me."

Ted watched the expressions on her face as he told her about his life with them. Surprise, shock, disbelief. All the same reactions he'd had. But he didn't tell her about the night a 'bo came after him with a knife, how Campy had shouted a warning to him, a warning that had saved him from what could have been a fatal slashing. It had given Ted the split second he'd needed to roll like a cannonball out of the drifter's path. But the blade still caught him in the right thigh. It had taken a doctor half the night to stitch him back together.

"I can't believe the lengths you'll go to for a story. Do you always do that?"

They'd reached the car and Ted opened the door for her. "Sometimes," he answered vaguely.

North of the downtown business district they passed into an area of darkened warehouses and aging derelict buildings. These were on the south bank of the Missouri River where Kansas City had had its beginnings. Some of the edifices were being turned into trendy artists' lofts, but most remained deserted with only their shells left to attest to a more flourishing era.

Ted turned down a deserted alleyway.

Kyla looked around. At night, the area had an eerie feel. "Are we safe here?"

"Relatively. Are you frightened?"

She reached out a hand and clutched his arm for reassurance. "If you're not, I'm not," she said, her answer a total bluff.

His eyes probed the dark, searching for things unseen as if he were equipped with some kind of radar. At last he found what he was looking for. "This is it. Armbruster Casket Works," he said, opening the car door.

"You're not getting out, are you?" She tightened her hold on his arm.

"You want to come with me?"

Her mind weighed the possibility against the option of remaining in the car alone. Neither appealed to her.

"Look, I'm just going over to the back of that building to check out a few things. I'll be back in a flash." He placed a hand over her tightening fingers.

Reluctantly, she let go of him.

"Lock your doors. You'll be safe."

She did as he suggested, then slid down in the seat to wait, her heart pounding. Reporters didn't have enough sense to be afraid, she thought with exasperation. They loved danger, courted it, placed themselves in situations other people avoided—like sinister alleyways and coffin factories at night. Minutes marched by, seeming like hours.

Then her eye caught a shadow. There was a sharp rap on the glass of the car window. Kyla's heart turned upside down and she gasped.

"Dammit, Spencer!" she croaked, barely able to get her voice around the tight knot of fright in her throat.

"Lemme in."

She reached over and released the lock. "You scared the life out of me."

"I'm sorry," he said, sliding into the seat beside her. "I didn't mean to frighten you."

He reached over and cupped her cheek. Kyla felt the roughness of his thumb abrade her lower lip. His mouth was close. She could feel its heat. Her own mouth trembled, wanting his kiss.

"You bewitch me, woman. You know that, don't you?" he whispered against the fullness of her lips. Warm shudders reverberated through her like shock waves. She wasn't sure who was bewitching whom.

The crashing sound of metal brought them to attention. Kyla's spine went rigid. "Ted, is someone out there?"

"Yes, and that someone's after Campy's belongings. I stashed them behind some metal containers and from the sound of things, they've just been found." He groped behind the seat for his Louisville Slugger, then flipped the switch on the dome light so it wouldn't come on when he opened the car door.

"You're not going out there, are you? Ted, you could get hurt." Her voice was laced with panic.

"I'll be fine." He opened the car door. "Lock this behind me and stay put. And don't worry. I know what I'm doing."

Kyla buried her face in her hands as he slid silently out of the car. This was insane—sitting in a darkened alleyway at two o'clock in the morning while Ted raced off into the night armed with a bat to protect the few paltry possessions of a vagrant.

She peered through the dark but could see only shadows. She strained her ears, but could only catch muffled sounds—someone running, indistinct voices on the night air, a train whistle in the distance, then silence.

Her imagination ran wild. Ted could be lying out there right now, injured. And she was doing nothing but cowering here in the car.

She remembered Ted's warning as she opened the car door, but she shoved it aside. Hesitantly, with her heart thudding loudly, she started down the alley in the direction Ted had taken. Her eyes began to adjust to the dark. The moon was three-quarters full, but it only cast a sinister pall over everything. Still, she could make out shapes—darkened buildings, lean-tos, Dumpsters.

A cat scurried across her path with a menacing squeal. Kyla gasped and waited for her heart to leave her throat. Where was Ted?

There...ahead of her...scuffling sounds. Ted? Footsteps...someone running...the sound growing fainter...then fading.

"I thought I told you to stay in the car."

Kyla jumped. He had come out of the shadows. "Do you have to scare me like that?"

"Scare you? I ought to take you over my knee." He tightened his grip on her arm and marched her toward the car.

"I was worried about you. What happened back there? I heard scuffling—"

"Just some bum after Campy's things. We tangled. He took off." Kyla noticed the old black trash bag he was dragging along behind him.

Campy's belongings? "Are you all right? He didn't hurt you...?" What could there be in that bundle worth risking his life for?

Ted was angry with her. He opened the car door and deposited her inside, then tossed the bundle in the trunk. "I can take care of myself, but when I have to look after you as well, that's a different story," he said, sliding in beside her.

"If you're waiting for me to say I'm sorry, you can keep on waiting. I won't apologize for being concerned about your safety."

Ted took her back to her car in the hospital lot, then saw her safely home. At her door he tipped her chin upward. "You really were worried about me?" he asked.

"Yes," she said softly.

Her answer wrapped around him like a warm blanket and brought a smile to his lips. She must care about his worthless hide in some small measure, he thought. "I'm sorry I was so rough on you."

"You're forgiven." His deep green eyes glistened in the moonlight that illuminated her doorstep. "Would you like to come in for hot chocolate?" she heard herself ask. What was she doing? It was late, and she had just thrown away what little bit of caution she had left.

"I'd love some."

7

KYLA CARRIED IN THE MUGS of hot chocolate, fixed her favorite way—topped with swirls of whipped cream. Ted sat tangled in thought at one end of her living room sofa, unaware that she'd even entered the room. Her gaze lingered for a moment on his profile. A captivating view. His bold slash of nose, his jaw set, they were like angry projections of volcanic rock. Was he still back in the alleyway, tormented by the hard life Kyla had but glimpsed tonight?

Just then he turned to her and the look softened.

"Your hot chocolate," she said, offering him his mug.

Ted smiled up at her, wrapping his hands around it. "Mmm, thanks. Smells good." And warm, he thought, like the carriage house, like this woman, curling up on the opposite end of the sofa, only one cushion away from him. She'd slipped off her shoes and tucked her feet up under the skirt of her white uniform. She took a sip of her drink, then licked the whipped cream off her top lip. He sucked in a breath. He'd have liked to have done that for her.

"What about the casket?" she asked, her eyes solemn as she looked up from her drink. "Was it all right?"

Ted fought down the hot desire knotting his insides, concentrating instead on her question. "For now. But I can't say for how long. When these people sleep under a piece of cardboard in a doorway, a casket is like a first-class hotel."

Kyla noticed his features harden like stone. She'd been right. He was upset by the events they'd found themselves caught up in tonight. "Aren't there places people like Campy can go for a meal, a bed?" she asked, feeling suddenly ignorant of the enormity of the problem. She'd treated many of the homeless in the ER, but turned them over to Social Services afterward, assuming that department would somehow rectify the situation.

"There are shelters, but the real diehards like Campy won't use them. They say they don't want to listen to all that ear-banging religion. In bad weather we—some of us from the paper—go out and try to round them up and get them into the Mission House or one of the other places for the night, but it's not easy. They'd rather stay out in the open. It's a hard life. Like the concrete around them—rough, cold, unforgiving."

Kyla sensed the melancholy in him, knew he needed to talk. She took another sip of her drink and waited for him to continue.

"At least I managed to salvage his stash. If I hadn't I might as well have hopped the next freight out of K.C." He played with the handle of his mug. "It was everything the poor codger owned in this world. A rusty coffeepot. A fork with two prongs missing. A few ragged clothes. The sum total of the man's existence. Hardly the crown jewels I was protecting."

He smiled at some private thought, then looked over at her, his green eyes dancing. "These people are not unhappy, though. They have friends they'd cut off their right arms for. At night around a bonfire there's a strong sense of camaraderie I've never found duplicated in the world we're familiar with."

Kyla recalled the magic she'd sensed between Ted and Campy and thought perhaps she understood just a little of what he meant. Now if only she could understand this puzzle of a man who sat here sipping hot chocolate with her, this man who'd lied his way into the ER a few short weeks ago. Was he the same man who'd befriended a poor street bum who smelled worse than a garbage dump in a stiff breeze, the same man who tore off down a deserted alleyway at night to retrieve the few worthless belongings of a friend?

It had been a strange evening, but then no evening she'd spent in Ted Spencer's company had exactly been ordinary.

"I'd better get out of here and let you get some sleep," he said, setting his mug down on the coffee table. He took her into his arms. She smelled so good, so fresh and female. "I'd love to undress you, Kyla Bradford, and search your body for every one of those freckles you have hidden beneath that uniform, but I'll settle for the taste of whipped cream on your lips—at least for tonight."

His voice was a husky whisper against her lips. Desire coiled low within her, fiery and hot and unquenchable. His breath was warm against her mouth as he inclined his head closer. His mouth searched for hers, his kiss stealing what little bit of air she had left in her lungs.

Her arms anchored around his neck as if he were a life preserver and she was drowning in a sea of passion that threatened to suck them both under.

He let out a low groan and dragged his mouth from hers, nibbling her lower lip as if he couldn't quite bring himself to free himself of her. "It's late and you need your sleep," he murmured, placing one final wet and wonderful kiss on her nose.

He snatched up his leather jacket from the chair where he'd tossed it when he'd arrived. "Oh, I just remembered. I have the pictures that Blood Hound took of you and your mom." He fumbled in the inside pocket of his coat. "I like her by the way. She's a neat lady—like her daughter." He found the pictures and handed them over. "I kept one for myself—of you in a pensive pose."

Kyla looked up at him as she took the pictures. He'd wanted a picture of her. She wished she had one of him, too.

He stole one last kiss from her and then he was gone. And she knew he'd taken her heart with him.

DESPITE HER LATE NIGHT, Kyla woke early. She had the day off and the hours loomed ahead of her endlessly. She couldn't put a name to the restlessness and she didn't try to. Instead, she dressed in casual slacks and a pullover sweater and backed her Mustang out of the driveway. There wasn't a cloud in the sky as she raced along the interstate. The sun was warm on her cheeks as it filtered through the windshield.

Although she hadn't set out with a plan in mind, she found herself at the hospital with a tiny bunch of flowers in her hand, knocking on Campy's door.

The lovable derelict appeared much better and was obviously enjoying his newfound life-style. Plumped against a stack of pillows, he was playing havoc with the television channels as he directed his remote control to do his bidding. Kyla wondered if he'd ever again be satisfied with a casket for a bed after this taste of relative luxury.

Finding a satisfactory channel at last, he laid the remote down and looked up, peering at his visitor. "Flowers?" he spluttered, scoffing at the multi-colored blooms. "What is this? Do I look dead?"

Kyla laughed and brushed at a spiky stalk of his silver-gray hair that his pillow had rearranged. "Not in the least. I found these in the trash can in the corridor and thought you might like them." She'd known that

Campy wouldn't respond easily to kindness, so she'd kept her tone mildly insulting.

"Get 'em out of here. I don't want no posies until I'm six foot under and can't smell 'em."

Ignoring him, Kyla arranged them in a specimen cup and set them on the windowsill within his range of vision. "You've got some pink in your cheeks this morning. Are you feeling better or is it just meanness I see?"

They sparred for a while, with the ill-mannered fellow eyeing her cagily. Then, as if realizing that the scrappy Kyla could match him barb for barb, he finally accepted her.

When Ted walked in a short time later, and saw Kyla rearranging the contents of Campy's luncheon tray for easier access and Campy allowing the fussing, he was certain he was seeing things. He glanced from one to the other and back again. "Are you two friends?"

"Don't look so shocked. The girl's all right in my book," Campy retorted. "Now, both of you clam up and let me eat in peace."

Ted's and Kyla's eyes met and locked, his full of surprised amusement, hers full of pleasure at seeing him again, an emotion she'd struggled against for a full ten seconds before giving in to it.

He was dressed casually in khaki slacks and a hunter green sweater that was only a shade darker than his eyes. His hair was an unruly tumble of curls, as if he'd let it dry that way after his morning shower. Kyla tried to put her mind on fast forward, past the thought of water jets sluicing over Ted's broad pectorals, his lean waist, his . . .

The room was warm, too warm. She looked away from him, certain her cheeks were as pink as ripe watermelon.

"Is this a nonmedical visit?"

Kyla looked up. His eyes swept over her, assessing her casual attire. She felt the blood rush to her cheeks again. She couldn't really say why she'd come, but looking at the man standing across the hospital bed from her, she had a fair idea he was a definite part of the reason. "I . . . I stopped by to see if Campy was all right, if he . . . needed anything."

Ted's voice was a low chortle. "From the looks of him, I'd say he's making out like a bandit."

Kyla's gaze swung to the patient, who was mopping up the last of the gravy from his plate of roast beef with a slice of bread, oblivious to the company in his room. "I'd say you're right."

She moved around the end of the bed. It was time to go. She was certain Campy and Ted had things to talk about. "I was just about to leave," she said. "I'll look in on him again tomorrow."

As she turned to tell Campy goodbye, Ted caught her hand. "Don't go." His look was pleading, his grasp enveloping and warm.

"I thought you two might . . . might need to talk. I'm sure he's worried about his belongings."

Ted looked over at the happy bum who was now immersing himself in a rich butterscotch pudding, with pure childish delight inscribed on his features. "Is that the face of a man who's worried?"

Kyla laughed. "At the moment, no."

The door to the room opened just then, and a nursing aide entered. She smiled at the visitors, then moved to the bedside. "Can I get you anything, Mr. McDuff?" she asked.

Campy's eyes lit up. "Got any more of these?" He waved an empty pudding dish in the air.

Ted turned to Kyla. "I don't think he needs either one of us. Come on, let's get out of here."

THE AFTERNOON was wild and crazy. Since neither of them had had lunch, Ted suggested carryouts from his favorite barbecue place, then found a park with a picnic table for their feast.

"Eat up," Ted urged when she was halfway through her plate of ribs. "There's a festival of Humphrey Bogart films at the Orpheum this afternoon and if we hurry we can catch the first one." He remembered she shared the same passion for old movies that he did, and what vintage movie buff could resist an afternoon of Bogie films!

She ordered Ted to help her polish off the remaining ribs, and they set off, laughing like two kids playing truant from school.

Slipping unseen over the green velvet cord roping off the stairs to the balcony, they settled into front row seats with their buttered popcorn and their jujubes.

Ted scrunched down in his seat to get more comfortable. "I don't know why they restrict this area. Old movies are best viewed from the balcony," he contended.

Kyla waved a hand at him. "Shh! It's starting."

The house lights dimmed and a hush fell over the sparsely filled theater. Kyla could feel her excitement build as the screen came alive with the larger-than-life characters. She leaned back in her red plush seat to let her senses fill with the make-believe drama unfolding before her.

She could lose herself for hours in a good film and *Casablanca* was the best. She knew nearly every line by heart, but still thrilled over each spoken word, each nuance, each bittersweet kiss.

Ted slid one arm around her shoulders, and she relaxed against it. In the isolated darkness of the balcony, with the exotic setting flickering on the screen before her, she felt as if she were slipping into a dreamworld, an illusion where everything was right and wonderful.

She shivered with the beauty of it.

"Are you cold?" Ted rubbed his broad hands up and down her arms to warm her.

"No, I'm fine."

"Sure?"

"Sure."

Ted pulled her into the circle of his arms, her back against his chest. She fit there so easily, so naturally, as if they were two parts of a perfect puzzle. He buried his nose in the velvet fragrance of her hair. "You smell good," he said. "Like flowers growing wild in the woods."

"Shh! We're missing the movie." In reality, Kyla could hardly concentrate on the film. She wanted to listen to the rumbly sound of Ted's voice as he whispered into her hair, sending shivers along her scalp like massaging fingers. She wanted to tell him he smelled wonderful too. Spicy and musky and male.

Her first instinct had been to run from this relationship, run as fast she could in the opposite direction. But somewhere along the way she had stumbled, and he had caught her, and she didn't seem to mind in the least. She could no longer picture him as the villain she'd originally believed him to be, the arrogant reporter who'd come into her life that night under less than commendable circumstances. Instead, he was thoughtful and gentle, funny and sad—and the sexiest man she'd ever known.

She slipped her hand into his, needing more of him. His palm was broad and warm. His fingers played with hers in an erotic dance, destroying all her powers of rational thought. Scenes from the picture staggered across the screen in one large blur. Even after having seen this movie dozens of times in the past, she had trouble following it now. She tried to keep her breathing even and slow, but her heart was hammering so loudly she was sure he could hear it.

Ted's mind had struggled for a while to focus on the movie, but instead he preferred to center his attention on the piece of action in his arms. She was real, oh so blissfully real—not an illusion. Since he'd met her, he hadn't been able to get her out of his mind. She plagued him, teased him, delighted him. He'd never felt like this before with any other woman, wanting to be near her every waking moment, thrilling at the sight of her, the sound of her voice, her touch. Everything about Kyla drove him wild.

Holding her in his arms in this empty balcony was exquisite torture. He wanted to slip his hand beneath her sweater, caress the smooth skin beneath it, but he knew that having to stop there would be even more agonizing. No, he wouldn't start something he couldn't finish. Not now, not here.

Instead, he tried to immerse himself in the movie, hoping the action of the scenes would drown the fires of passion that Kyla had set.

And for a while it worked.

Until the love scene.

The passion on the screen only increased his acute awareness of the woman he held in his arms. "Let's get out of here," he said when he was able to endure no more. His voice cracked with desire.

"Now?" The huge gray eyes she turned on him were questioning.

He shrugged his shoulders. "This part always makes me cry."

She laughed lightly. The sound reminded him of water trickling over stones in a mountain stream.

He waited while she gathered up her purse, then they crept down the balcony stairs, smiled broadly at the usher as they climbed over the velvet rope and made their escape out into the bright sunlight.

"Spencer, you're incorrigible, waltzing past that usher as if you owned the theater."

"You're as irreverent as I am. Don't forget, you were right there beside me."

They ran, laughing, to the car. He held the door for her while she slid in, then hurried around to the driver's side.

"Let's face it, Kyla, we're both rogues." He leaned over and kissed her mouth, abandoning himself to the delightful taste of her lips. "If this wasn't Main Street and broad daylight, lady..." he whispered against them

Kyla's flailing emotions echoed his words. She took a deep measured breath to clear her head. She'd always kept the dates she'd had cool and uncomplicated, but this man threatened to turn her life inside out. He had the power to steal her heart. With each moment she spent in his company, each look he gave her, each kiss, she was digging herself in deeper.

He was heading south on Main, whipping the car through the heavy daytime traffic. "Where are we going?" she asked, realizing he was not taking her back to her car in the hospital lot.

He took his eyes from the road and looked over at her, giving her a lopsided grin. "I have some popcorn left and I know a couple of ducks who really like this stuff."

Sounds safe enough, she decided, and leaned back in her seat to relax. The wind riffled through her hair and the sun warmed her face, banishing all thought from her mind.

Soon they reached the park. Ted found a place to leave the car, and they sauntered toward the duck pond. He caught at her hand, but Kyla lifted it to sweep a windswept tendril from her eyes, carefully evading his touch. She had to try to keep him at a safe distance because he was muddling her senses again.

When they reached the pond, Ted bent down at the edge of it and scattered a few kernels of popcorn onto the water's surface. Two ducks skimmed by and greedily snatched them up. Soon they were joined by several more, all demanding their share.

"Here, see if they'll take some from you." Ted offered Kyla some of the popcorn.

As one duck swam near, Kyla held out her hand. He eyed her curiously at first, then snatched the morsel with a sharp peck of his beak. Ted laughed as Kyla jerked her hand away. "That wasn't funny, Spencer. I think I've been mortally wounded."

"Let me see." He grasped her hand before she could pull it away. "Just as I thought. Not a mark. But perhaps a kiss will make it feel better."

His lips brushed across her palm, sending erotic messages to her very core, dangerous messages. She shivered, then jerked her hand away. "Better already. But I don't recall seeing that procedure in a first-aid book."

"You didn't read the chapter 'How to Treat Duck Bites.'"

Kyla laughed. "I must have missed that one," she said, thinking Ted's treatment could prove dangerous if administered too often. Perhaps even fatal to the faint of heart.

The sun was warm through the crisscrossing branches of the trees, the breeze light and airy, causing barely a ripple on the pond. A perfect day, Kyla thought as she settled onto a park bench to watch Ted toss out the last remaining popcorn to the feathered flotilla.

When he was finished giving out the snack, Ted slid onto the bench beside her. "Tell me, what was it like growing up in Smalltown, U.S.A.?" he asked.

"*Lewis*town," she retorted. "And it's not so small. We have a traffic light and everything."

He feigned an apologetic look and waited for her to continue.

"I grew up on the edge of town in a big white two-story house. The orchard was out behind. It's beautiful in the spring when the trees are in bloom. White apple blossoms for as far as the eye can see."

"I'd like to see it sometime."

She turned away, her gaze following the ducks. She'd like to show it to him, she realized. Very much.

He played with a tendril of her hair, slowly winding the wisp around his finger. "Tell me about the orchard."

"I thought my mother gave you enough information to write a book on the subject." She turned laughing eyes on him.

His own smiled back. "I want to hear you tell it."

"I don't know what I can add. My brothers and I picked apples, sprayed trees, made cider, operated the roadside stand. There was always something to do around the place—either work or play. We had a horse in the back pasture that we rode sometimes—when the old gal was in the mood, that is. And there's a stream bisecting the property where we used to fish."

"The only girl among three boys? I'm sure you were spoiled rotten."

"I was not! My brothers used to tease me unmercifully. I had to scrap and fight back—" She broke off, feeling she'd said something wrong, but not sure what. Ted had suddenly gotten to his feet, his hands jammed into his pockets, scuffing the toe of his shoe at a clump of grass. "Anyway, it wasn't always so great having brothers," she finished lamely.

Ted turned back to look at her, stroking her face with his eyes. "I'd say you were pretty lucky." Kyla had just described what he'd missed as a child, the family he would have loved to have had. Perhaps one day he would have it—for his children.

"I've babbled on enough. Now tell me about Ted Spencer," she said.

Ted returned to the bench. "Your turn's not up. I want to know more—such as, how did you get all those freckles your mother talked about?"

She laughed. "Skinny-dipping in the stream."

His gaze inched over various parts of her body. "These freckles—you must have them in interesting places."

"Embarrassing places." How had this conversation gone so awry in such a short span of time? she wondered.

His hands burrowed beneath her hair, his fingertips feather dancing sensuously along the nape of her neck. "I'd like to try skinny-dipping with you in that stream sometime," he murmured.

"Can't." Her breath felt as if it were trapped in her chest.

He lowered his head, his mouth seeking hers. "Can't?"

"Too shallow now."

His lips were a whisper's distance from hers. "That's a pity."

"Still good fishing though."

"Not as much fun."

"No."

He parted her lips, his tongue dipping and tasting the warmth within. She was a surprise package that he longed to open, slowly untying the ribbon, then the gift wrapping. He could only imagine the treasure that awaited inside.

Kyla gave herself up to the glory of sensations exploding within her. She wanted this man; she could no longer deny it. Desire hummed in her veins like sweet music.

She pressed her breasts against his chest, needing his heat, craving his closeness. Only he could stop the ache building within her.

Ted heard the noise first. A faint rustling sound. He'd thought it was the wind eddying the leaves at his feet. But it wasn't timed with the riffling of leaves still clinging to the trees. Reluctantly, he dragged his mouth from Kyla's. Still holding her close he looked down.

"Quack!"

He and Kyla broke into laughter. One of the ducks had waddled over from the pond, and was investigating the empty popcorn box for leftovers.

"Your timing's lousy, guy," Ted told the greedy creature. "I'm busy seducing this lady and your interruption is not appreciated. Now, shoo." He waved a hand at the duck.

"Quack, quack!" The creature stood his ground.

"It's his park," Kyla said, wiping tears of laughter from her eyes. "I think we're the interruption."

"*Us?* We were sitting here minding our own business—"

"Come on, Spencer." She stood up, dragging him to his feet as he continued to protest his right to be there. "I'll fix us a couple of hamburgers."

She didn't want to end this day with Ted—not just yet. It was too perfect. He was too perfect. His laughter. His kisses. Even his . . . seduction. It might be interesting to see just where he intended to go with that, she thought with a smile.

"SO THEY WERE A LITTLE PINK on the inside," Ted said, describing the hamburgers he'd cooked on the grill. "They weren't that bad."

"A little pink? Fuchsia would be closer to the truth," Kyla taunted as they cleared away the remains of their impromptu dinner. "Not to mention charred on the outside. I thought you said burgers were your specialty."

"If you hadn't kept distracting me with that tempting body of yours..." He swatted her sexy bottom with the end of his dish towel.

"A poor excuse, Spencer."

"No excuse. You drive me crazy, you know that, don't you?" He caught her around the neck with his flying dish towel and pulled her to him. "Take back what you said about my culinary skills."

"And if I don't?"

"You have to kiss the cook."

"Your hamburgers were—" she wanted his kisses, couldn't get enough of them "—positively dreadful."

"That does it!"

Ted's mouth came down hard on hers, exacting punishment, then it gentled into something sensual, something far more devastating. Kyla felt the temperature in her tiny kitchen soar twenty degrees.

Her legs felt like Jell-O. She leaned into him for support. This man was turning her world topsy-turvy, and she wasn't sure she could set it back on its axis—or that she wanted to. She was beginning to enjoy looking at life this way, the way Ted did, slightly out of kilter.

He drew back, his green eyes brushing her face. "Let's finish our wine in front of the fire."

"Mmm. Sounds nice."

Slipping an arm around her waist he led her into the living room. Kyla felt the sudden loss of warmth when he released her to tend to the fire that had burned low. He knelt on one knee before the old stone fireplace, stoking the embers back to life. The firelight played on his skin, turning it golden. His muscles bunched and knotted beneath his sweater as he leaned forward to add a log. He rocked back on his heels, watching until it caught, then he joined Kyla on the floor in front of it.

She nestled in the crook of his arm and took a sip of her wine, feeling warm and glowing and knowing the feeling had everything to do with the man beside her. "When I was a kid I liked to find shapes in the flames," she said, studying the fire.

"Me, too. One of my favorite pastimes. There," he pointed. "See it, a dancing elephant."

"Didn't see it. Are you sure it's not the wine?"

He gave her a pained look. "The whole idea is to let your imagination loose."

"I know that, but I still didn't see an elephant. Sorry."

"Well, your turn. Tell me what you see."

Kyla watched the orange flames dart and flicker rhythmically in front of her, finding no distinguishable shapes at first. "There—a couple doing the funky chicken," she exclaimed, pointing wildly.

"The funky chicken?"

"You said, use my imagination . . ."

He ruffled her hair. "Oh, Kyla, will I ever get enough of you?" His voice had gone from playful to soft in the space of one sentence.

Kyla trembled. "I hope not," she murmured. She traced his bottom lip with a fingertip. "When I first met you, Ted Spencer, I wasn't at all sure I liked you. I thought you were arrogant and inconsiderate of other people's feelings. You were a reporter, no better than the ones who hang around the ER night after night. Oh, you made my heart flutter—I won't deny that. But I didn't want to get to know you, I didn't want you in my life...."

"And now?" he asked gently.

She drew her hand away from his face and watched the flames lick at the burning log in the grate. "I've revised my opinion. You are a very feeling, very caring person. When I saw you with Campy—"

Ted touched her chin, turning her face toward him. "Forget that. I meant, do you want me in your life now?"

Her answer was a whisper, falling from her lips like a gentle rain. "Yes."

He smiled and raised her hand to his lips, kissing the soft pad of each fingertip. "When I met *you*, Kyla Bradford, I was convinced you were no angel of mercy. You know, you weren't very nice to me."

"I know."

"From that first night I couldn't get you off my mind. You fascinated me and made me furious at the same time. A very disturbing combination of feelings. But I kept showing up at the hospital hoping to see you."

"Why?"

He played with her hair, winding one silken strand around his finger. The scent of it, of her, was driving him wild. "Why? I asked myself that question dozens of times."

"And?"

"And I couldn't come up with an answer. But I've never felt like this about a woman before. You've done this to me, Kyla. It's all your fault."

She laughed softly, then her eyes darkened, her face growing contemplative. "There's...there's been no one, no one serious, in your life?"

Ted's mind flickered back to the one time he'd thought there was. Now he knew there'd been no one who even came close to making him feel the way Kyla made him feel. "No one," he answered. "But what about you? You must have broken male hearts from the moment you first tried out that smile."

Kyla laughed gently. "Maybe one or two over the years, but I'm sure they recovered quite nicely."

"And lately?"

"Lately?" Only Ted, she thought to herself, realizing how very important he'd become to her. "The ER keeps me busy, so I don't have many free evenings for dating."

He grazed a finger along her cheek. "I intend to claim every one of those free evenings and any other time I can get. I want to be with you, Kyla."

Kyla smiled. "I'd like that. Very much."

He tilted her chin up, brushing his thumb across the fullness of her lips, fighting the urges screaming inside his body. He wanted Kyla. His need for her was killing him. "I want to kiss you, here in front of the fire, but I'm afraid I won't stop."

"Then don't, Spencer."

"Don't kiss you?"

"Don't stop."

Ted read the invitation in her eyes, her slightly parted mouth. He took the wineglasses and set them aside. She looked so beautiful in the firelight. He would love her slowly, thoroughly, until she was ready for him. His heart thundered against his ribs and his body hardened with want and need—need for this one woman.

"Kyla," he whispered her name—a plea, a prayer—as his hands tangled in her loose auburn hair and his head lowered to hers.

Her lips were warm and waiting, yielding under his. His tongue delved inside her mouth, and she met it with her own need and passion, hungrily, eagerly. They tasted and savored and explored, learning each other. Passion licked at them as hot as the fire burning in the grate.

Ted dropped kisses along her neck, his tongue dipping into the hollow of her throat, tasting her skin's saltiness. "You have too many clothes on for me to do this properly," he said.

Kyla smiled and reached for the hem of her sweater to pull it over her head.

"No, let me." He put his hands on hers, stopping their progress, then slowly lifted the garment off.

He unfastened the clasp of her white lacy bra and discarded it. Her breasts fell into his hands with a soft weight. Firelight danced over her nakedness, painting her skin a golden hue.

"You are so beautiful," he murmured and lowered his head to kiss the rosy peaks of her breasts.

His tongue stroked each one in turn until the sensitive buds hardened into taut nubs. He suckled and sipped as if he'd never get his fill of her. Kyla clung to his neck, her fingers kneading it, as a purr of pleasure broke from her throat.

Reluctant to leave the nectar of her breasts, Ted found the closure of her slacks and undid them, then slid them down her slender hips. His hands caressed her bare skin with trembling reverence before he slipped off the white wisp of her panties.

The Greeks could never have sculpted a woman's form to this perfection, he thought. He wanted to tell her so, but he was certain he wouldn't be able to get the words out in a coherent sentence. Instead, he'd tell her with his touch, with his lips.

He bent to brush a kiss across her thigh, but Kyla stopped him. Her eyes were dark with desire. He saw the hunger in them and knew her need, her longing, matched his own.

"You have too many clothes on, Spencer." She repeated his words of a few moments before.

He laughed softly and quickly moved to shed them.

"No, let me," she murmured.

She seemed to take extraordinary delight in baring each part of him to her smoldering gaze, her eyes lingering in fascination and pleasure as she worked on the various fasteners. Her fingers toyed and caressed, branding him with her touch. His skin sang beneath her explorations. His muscles tensed and relaxed, then tensed again. She was slowly driving him mad.

Spencer was glorious, Kyla thought, running a reverent hand over the crinkly dark hairs on his thigh. All hardness and muscle and . . . His desire for her was evident in his full arousal. It was a heady feeling. Her hand found its way into the dark tangle of hair on his chest. "You are a beautiful man," she whispered. "And I want you."

He wanted to take her then, drive his manhood into her, make her his finally and irrevocably, but with sheer willpower he held himself in check. Making love with Kyla must be a celebration.

"And I want you," he murmured. "All of you, every inch of you."

Kyla drew in a shaky breath as his lips caressed a path over her burning skin, finding each erogenous spot and many she didn't realize had that quality. He brought her alive to a quivering awareness she'd never thought herself capable of. Her fingers bit into the hard muscles of his shoulders. "Love me, Ted," she whispered.

"Patience, my love. I haven't found all the freckles yet."

That's what he was doing? Kissing his way along the path of her freckles? She cursed the fact that the sun had bestowed so many on her body. He'd aroused her to a flash point. She wanted him now.

"One hundred and twelve," he murmured, raising his head to study the smoky haze of desire in her eyes. "Freckles," he added, seeing her questioning look.

Then his mouth closed over hers in a kiss that was long and deep. His hands stroked her, and she touched him, nearly making him explode. He removed her hand. Another moment of that and he'd be finished.

Levering himself over her, he slipped into her. He moved slowly and rhythmically, pleasing her, pleasing himself. He watched the play of emotions on her face, as primitive in their need as his. His pace increased and Kyla matched it, raising her hips, drawing him in deeper.

"Kyla!" He caroled her name as passion drove them on, spiraling, soaring, taking them to heights neither had ever experienced before.

"Yes, oh, yes," she answered back as shock wave after shock wave shuddered through her.

Then Ted plunged one final time, filling her with all he had to give before he collapsed against her, his breathing as ragged as hers. Moments later their heartbeats slowed, their breathing returned to normal. Neither noticed the chill to their perspiration-slick bodies.

Kyla had never felt so sated, so loved. She snuggled into the crook of his arm, wrapped in the warmth and the scent of their lovemaking. She loved this man. She knew there would never be anyone else for her.

8

TED'S WARM LIPS NIPPING her earlobe nudged Kyla into wakefulness. She forced open one eye, then closed it against the bright sunlight that streamed through the window. Sometime during the night he'd carried her to bed and they'd made love again. She smiled, remembering.

"Do you always sleep this late?" His voice was a velvet purr beside her ear.

She turned toward him and opened her eyes, letting them brush across his unshaven face and mischievous green eyes. "Every chance I get." This man made the idea of morning seem somehow tolerable. "What time is it?"

"Time to rise and shine."

Good Lord. Spencer was an early riser. Why hadn't she thought to find that out *before* she fell in love with him? *Not smart, Bradford,* she chided herself.

Love. That was another problem. Dammit! She had not intended to fall in love. The very thought frightened her to death. But it was too late now.

And Ted? What about his feelings toward her? Last night he'd certainly made her feel loved, like she was the most important thing in his life, but he hadn't said the words.

"There's makings for French toast in the kitchen," she said, snuggling down into the covers. "This is my day off."

"All the more reason not to waste a minute of it."

Kyla opened her eyes a slit to see if he was serious. He was. "Do you have to go into the paper?"

"Not until later."

"Then come back to bed."

He feathered kisses across her cheek. "That's a very tempting offer, but I have a better one."

Kyla couldn't imagine anything better than making love with Ted in this already warm bed. Before she could ask what he had in mind, he scooped her up in his arms and flung her over his shoulder.

"Ted Spencer, put me down." She pummeled his back with blazing fists.

"This is the only way to get you out of bed, sleepyhead. An early morning shower will get you going." He paraded across the room with her like she were a sack of flour.

"Don't you dare, Spencer. Don't you dare. I'll get you for this." Kyla wasn't ready for the harsh reality of water peppering her backside on a chilly morning. She gave her warm bed a look of longing as he carried her away from it.

Her threat was met with a hearty cackle as he carried her toward the bathroom. He began to sing as he angled into the shower stall and turned on the water, carefully adjusting the controls. A bouncy little song— the kind of ditty only morning people sang.

"Ted, my hair . . . I'll get wet." She pounded his back again, feeling like a fly annoying a sumo wrestler.

"That's what generally happens in a shower."

She was soaked in seconds as Ted put her under the nozzle's spray. He stood her on her feet and water sluiced over her. Her hair clumped into sodden tangles that she was certain resembled seaweed.

She looked up at him, then at the shower door, gauging her chance of escape, then back at him. Water drizzled over his head, turning his brown curls into tight ringlets. His body glistened like dewdrops on a misty morning. His hand reached for her. With one finger he traced the delicate skin of one breast, outlining its contour, then he took the same path along the other.

She wasn't going anywhere.

His mouth hovered an inch above hers. She gave a small gasp of anticipation, then closed the distance between them. His lips were wet and wild, sliding over hers in a sensuous drenching of liquid heat. His hands glided easily over the slickness of her skin. He cupped her bottom and drew her against his aroused body.

Kyla whispered his name against his lips. The heat of their breath mingled.

Finding the soap turning to suds in the small lake of the soap dish, he lathered her shoulders, her back, her breasts, the flare of her hips. Every one of her nerve endings screamed from his sweet torture.

"What a wonderful way to wake up," she murmured against his shoulder. She clung to his neck, her legs like two fragile stems of wheat in a rainstorm.

"I want to experience loving you in every erotic way I can think of, Kyla. I don't think I can ever get enough of you."

"I'll never get enough of you, either," she whispered, her own mind conjuring up a few suggestions of its own for loving this man. She captured the soap from his hand, and with gentle swirls, slid the creamy bar over his body, watching the suds foam into tiny peaks as she went.

He shuddered and a low guttural sound tore from his throat. "All my erogenous zones are clean, woman. You didn't miss one."

She dropped the bar of soap unceremoniously as he lifted her above him, whispering words of endearment before lowering her down onto his aroused readiness. Their wet bodies fused, sliding into a glorious union.

"Your water bill will be horrendous," Ted murmured when they collapsed against each other at last, their passion spent.

"It's one bill I'll pay with a smile on my face," she answered, "and a hot blush on my cheeks."

He laughed and kissed her lightly on the nose. "Now, how about a dry towel and a hot breakfast in that order. I think you mentioned something about makings for French toast. If you think I make a mean hamburger, wait until you see what I can do with bread and syrup."

AFTER THEIR HEARTY BREAKFAST they opted for a walk in the park. They strolled along in comfortable silence, their fingers linked. The air was crisp and fresh. Fall had disappeared, winter's chill replacing it, but Kyla felt warm inside. Never before had she opened herself up to a man—not like she had with Ted. But Ted seemed to demand that of her. She smiled, thinking of their togetherness of the past two days.

Ted had insisted on bringing along bread crumbs for the ducks. He knelt now at the edge of the pond, tossing them tidbits.

Kyla had a sudden image of him as a small boy, his tousled brown head intent on some task, as he was now. "What was your childhood like?" she asked as she bent beside him to watch the ducks eat from his hand.

He looked up at her and for a moment she thought he wasn't going to answer. "Lonely." He gave a philosophical shrug. "I was an only child. I had to make my own fun."

Her eyes searched his face but she found no bitterness there, only a faint sadness.

"I lived near here. In fact, this place used to be one of my favorite haunts." He smiled.

"Did you hate being an only child very much?" she asked, tossing a bread crumb to the duck.

He was silent for a moment, then nodded. "I used to lie awake at night and dream about having brothers and sisters, a fun, laughing family—like yours, Kyla. We lived in a huge house over there, off Ward Parkway." He pointed to the west, opposite the park. "My parents still live there. A big, silent, cold house I now laughingly call a mausoleum. I used to stand in the entry hall and let out a whoop, and the echoes would bounce off the walls. It made it sound like there were other kids there, shouting back. At least for a while—then it would be quiet again. I think it was the quiet I hated the most."

Absently, he tossed more crumbs to the ducks. "My father was always too busy for me. He spent much of his time on the phone, talking to his broker. He was a rich man, but he wanted more. No matter how much power and wealth he had, it was never enough for him."

Kyla remembered Ted's sneering remarks about Leonard Daniels's wealth, his own indifference to the family money that had apparently come his way—perhaps through a trust fund—and thought she understood just a little. She tried to picture his father, the home, the wealth, all so different from what she was used to. There'd been no mistaking the hurt she saw in Ted's face.

"What about your mother?" Kyla asked.

"She tried to be both mother and father to me, tried to make us feel like a family, but it wasn't the same."

Kyla thought of her brothers, the summer fun they'd shared, the hectic holidays and birthdays. "No, I suppose not."

Ted turned to her. He framed her face between his hands and bent his head to kiss her. Her heart quickened as his lips crushed hers, hard and insistent. Then, he turned and looked out across the pond as if concentrating on the ripples the wind was creating on its mirrored surface.

"One day I want a house filled with all the noise and laughter half a dozen rowdy kids can generate," he said, a smile replacing the sadness and hurt of a moment before.

Kyla felt like someone had tied a stone around her heart. Of course he would want children. And someday he would have a wife who would give them to him. A pain, wide and deep, seared through her as she pictured Ted with a woman, a woman touching him in that secure and comfortable way wives do.

She saw him surrounded by children, all of them little images of himself. He'd be a perfect father, she realized, giving each one the time and attention and love that had been denied him.

Kyla studied the bare limbs of the oak tree as they climbed toward the warmth of the sun. She kept her face averted, fearing that the pain and anguish in her heart would show in her eyes. She'd fallen in love with a man who wanted more from life than she could offer and she didn't know what to do about it.

KYLA SAT at the nursing station, making a necklace out of paper clips. For the past two days she'd pondered the situation in which she found herself. She had no future with Ted. That painful fact played over and over in her mind. He wanted a full-fledged family, to surround himself with life and laughter. He wanted to blot out the loneliness of his childhood.

The woman Ted chose to love for a lifetime should be someone who could share that future, not a woman who could not risk pregnancy. From the day the doctors had explained the inherent danger of her rheumatoid condition, Kyla realized pregnancy was not an option for her. She would never risk inviting the disease that had nearly incapacitated her.

"Why don't you take a break, Kyla." Roger lifted the chain of silver paper clips from her busy fingers. "Get yourself a cup of coffee. And make it decaf."

She didn't feel like taking a break, but she wasn't accomplishing very much here. "I'll be in the cafeteria if you need me."

Instead of taking the winding corridor to the cafeteria, Kyla rode the elevator to the fourth floor. Pediatrics was busy at this time of night. The nurses were readying the children for bed, administering bedtime medications, gathering up the toys the ambulatory youngsters had strewn along the hallway.

"What are you doing here, stranger?" Millie, one of the floor nurses, asked, picking up a stuffed teddy bear that had one ear missing. "It must be quiet in Emergency."

"It is," Kyla said. Too quiet. A hectic night would have kept her thoughts off of Ted and their hopeless situation.

"Well, anytime you want a transfer..."

"I'll keep it in mind." Working with children was very satisfying, she knew. She remembered her student nursing days in Peds. She'd loved the kids, the work. But she wasn't at all sure she could handle the constant reminder that she would never have any children of her own. A selfish reason for not choosing the department, perhaps, but a protective one. She smiled at Millie. "Can I put this to bed with one of the kids?" she asked, reaching for the bear Millie cradled in her arms.

A nurturer by instinct, Millie wasn't embarrassed to be caught cuddling the stuffed toy. "Benjamin. He's having a bone graft in the morning and he's frightened," she answered. "He fell out of a tree this summer and fractured his arm. It didn't heal."

Kyla found Benjamin huddled in the middle of the bed, a soft cast on his left arm. He looked as if he was about three or four years old, with large brown eyes and dark curls. Twin streaks of tears coursed down his rounded cheeks. "Are you gonna give me a shot?" he asked, his eyes growing wider.

Kyla read the fright in them. "No, Benjamin, I'm not. I just thought you could use a friend." She waggled the bear at him.

He studied her for a moment as if weighing out whether or not he could trust her, then he snatched the animal and tucked it tightly under his right arm. Shyly, he buried his face in the covers.

"My name's Kyla. I'd like to be your friend, too. Do you think that would be okay?"

There was silence for a moment, then she heard a muffled, "Guess so." Slowly, his face emerged from under the blankets and he peered out at her.

"I thought we could talk about what's going to happen in the morning—if you want, that is."

"Are you gonna op . . . op'rate on me?"

"No, but I know all about 'op'rations.'"

"You do?" His eyes grew wide.

Kyla's voice was soft, reassuring, and Benjamin responded. Fears only a four-year-old could imagine bubbled to the surface. She let him express them, then she took them one by one and explained everything to him in terms he could understand. While she talked, he hugged the bear tightly.

"And when I wake up my arm'll be all better?"

"Almost. You'll have to wear a cast for a little while longer. Think you can do that?"

He frowned. "Guess so."

Kyla brushed a curl back from his forehead. It was soft and springy. Her heart wrenched at just the touch. "Now, why don't you and Bear snuggle down into the covers and get some sleep." She leaned over and kissed him lightly on the cheek.

As she hurried out of the room and down the darkened corridor, she wondered why she had come. Tears stung her eyes. For the first time, she questioned the decision she'd made years ago. For the first time, she wondered whether her nursing career really would be enough for her.

She avoided the elevator that would be crowded now with departing visitors and took the stairs back down to Emergency, her world, a world that was familiar to her.

TED CIRCLED HIS DESK for the third time, paused, stared at the phone for a full minute, then changed direction.

"Is this a ceremony to ward off evil spirits or a new dance step?" Blood Hound asked, entering the nearly deserted newsroom and observing his friend's ritualistic pacing.

Ted looked up. "Huh? Oh, I . . . I was just . . ."

"Thinking?"

"Yeah, thinking."

"About a story."

"Yeah, a story," Ted answered, a slight edge to his voice. "Haven't you got something to do, Blood Hound?" He wanted to get back to his thoughts, dismal though they were. He had to figure out why Kyla was . . . avoiding him. There was no other word for it.

Something was wrong. He could feel it in his gut. Each time he'd talked to Kyla over the past few days, she'd reduced their conversations to a discussion of the weather or something else inconsequential. Hardly the conversations of a man and woman who had made glorious love together, sharing each other in the most special way possible.

Ted frowned as Blood Hound idly toyed first with the paperweight on the desk, then with the stapler. When he reached for the Garfield mug that served as a pencil caddy, Ted exploded. "Oh, for Pete's sake, Blood Hound, go play with your lens cap and leave me alone."

"You know, Spencer, you're a real bear tonight." Blood Hound lifted his chin to indicate his pique, then shuffled off.

Ted was left to brood. He wanted to phone Kyla again. His fingers itched to dial the ER's number. He glanced at the clock on the far wall. 10:45 p.m. She'd be off duty soon. Maybe he should just show up and take her for coffee. They could talk about whatever it was that was bothering her.

Yeah. That's what he'd do. He jerked his arms into his jacket sleeves and headed for the door. But before he reached it the phone jangled on his desk, shattering the quiet in the newsroom.

He thought twice about answering, then reached for the receiver. It could be important. "Spencer," he barked into the instrument. He glanced at the clock again. He didn't want to miss Kyla.

KYLA HEARD the Code Blue page. Her heart leapt into her throat as the room number registered in her mind.

"No, please, no," she pleaded with a higher authority. Campy was due to leave the hospital in the morning. He was better, much better.

The ER doctor and nurse reported to a code as well as the respiratory therapist, house resident and several other key staff members.

"I'll take it," Kyla announced to Leah. "You stay and mind the store." She was out the door in seconds, close on Roger's heels.

Campy's face was ashen, his body unresponsive when they reached the scene. His plump chest sported wire monitoring devices. A respiratory therapist was inserting an airway. A nurse was trying to get an IV going.

Kyla swallowed the knot in her throat and flew into action. A code had one of two possible outcomes—the patient survived or the patient died. Campy had to survive; she wouldn't allow the alternative.

"I'm not getting a blood pressure. Respiration's shallow and 45," she said, her voice sharp and clear, belying her anxiety.

"Heart's in arrest," Roger shouted, as Campy's heartbeat skated across the screen in a wide, abnormal pattern. "We'll have to shock him."

Kyla coated the paddles of the defibrillator with paste, then swiftly applied them to Campy's chest. Her hands didn't shake, but her heart was hammering. She checked the machine with a quick glance. "Stand clear," she ordered and delivered the charge to Campy's life-less body.

Everyone in the small room watched the screen, hoping, praying. The thin green line staggered across it in the same dangerous pattern.

"Again," Roger ordered.

"Clear," Kyla shouted as once more she applied the paddles. Please, God, she begged.

All eyes flew to the screen. The seconds ticked by. The aberrant line flickered, then steadied.

"We've got ourselves a normal rhythm." The relief in Roger's voice echoed that of the rest of them. Then he quickly gave the staff the necessary instructions.

Kyla released her pent-up breath. Campy had survived.

TED'S FACE WAS PALE, his hair ruffled as if he'd been rak-ing his fingers through it. Kyla's heart lurched at the sight of him. For a moment all she could think of was the feel of his arms around her, the warmth and texture of his lips as they brushed across her skin. For a mo-ment she was happy, everything was right between them—as it had been a few nights before.

Then she remembered the way things really were and a cold ache lodged near her heart. She could help bring someone back from the brink of death, but she could not solve what was wrong between them, no matter how much she wanted to.

"I'm glad the hospital reached you," she said. "Campy's stable. We're transporting him to Cardiac Care, where he can be monitored." Her words were crisply efficient, leaving everything she was feeling inside unsaid.

Ted released a ragged breath. Campy had pulled through! "Thanks," he whispered. "That doesn't begin to express half the gratitude I feel, but it's all I can think to say at the moment."

He'd heard the formal tone in her voice and hoped it was only because they were standing in the middle of the hospital corridor. For that reason, and that reason alone, he didn't haul her into his arms. She looked so enchantingly beautiful with her hair springing loose from her French braid and her cheeks shining with the glow of tonight's success.

Ted stepped back as the rest of the code team emerged from the room to transport their patient to the Cardiac Care Unit. He sucked in a breath as they wheeled Campy past, and Kyla realized he hadn't been prepared for what he'd see. The pallor, the tubes, the wires and electrodes. She put a hand on his shoulder, feeling the knot of tension beneath her fingers.

"He'll be all right," she murmured and gave him a bright, reassuring smile. She wanted to slip into his arms, breathe in his familiar scent, touch her lips to his. But she couldn't, not now, not ever again. She had to forget that she loved him, had to put him out of her mind and out of her life. How could she continue to see him, knowing one day, probably one day soon, he'd be ready to choose a wife—a wife who could be a mother to his children. "I . . . I have to go now," she said and hurried away.

She caught up to the others moving quickly toward the bank of elevators. Because of the very real possibility that the patient could arrest a second time, the code team always made the transfer to the Cardiac Care Unit. She hoped that would not happen. She doubted Campy could survive another heart attack in his weakened condition. As the elevator began to move she squeezed the old fellow's hand. His roughened fingers closed over hers and he smiled at her with his eyes before fatigue forced them shut again.

A month ago she didn't even know Campy; she didn't know Ted; and now they were both a vital part of her life. She leaned back against the wall of the elevator and squeezed her eyes shut. "Oh, Ted . . . ," she whispered and fought back her tears.

9

A FEW DAYS LATER, Campy was sitting up and sassing the nurses. His orneriness had returned—a sure sign of recovery. The CCU nurses were counting the days until they could ship him out of intensive care. A cardiology resident had visited that morning to explain the changes in life-style that were needed to avoid a second heart attack and left wearing the patient's chocolate milk on the front of his starched white lab coat.

When Kyla looked in on Campy later that same morning, he was still in a perverse mood. But in spite of his testiness, she knew he was glad to see her. They were friends—and they understood each other.

"I've been hearing complaints about you," she said as she breezed in, feeling a relief of sorts that Ted was not around. He hadn't, in fact, been around for the past two days and that puzzled her. Where was he? And why wasn't he looking in on Campy? He loved the old fellow. If Campy was curious about Ted's absence, he wasn't showing it. And she did not intend to bring it up. There was no sense getting him upset. She reached for the oxygen mask he sported on the top of his head and placed it firmly over his nose and mouth. "That won't do you any good up there."

"Can't stand the blamed thing," he groused, shoving it back up. "And what do you mean, complaints? I'd like to see any one of them hospital types lay in this bed, and put up with the abuse they heap on me."

Kyla considered chiding him about the chocolate milk incident but decided it would only rile him more—something he didn't need while his heart mended. In fact, she wondered how he'd come by the milk in the first place. She was certain it wasn't on a low cholesterol diet. Probably browbeat one of the nurses into bringing it to him. "You're doing so well you'll be going to another room soon, where the rules aren't so stringent."

"Rules," he snorted. "Never believed in 'em." But he looked pleased, nonetheless. "The doctor said I was lucky my ticker gave out while I was here in the hospital instead of on the streets, or I'd be pushin' up daisies right now." He gave a braying laugh. "Always was a lucky cuss."

Kyla saw no humor in his comment. He would need a great deal of luck if he had to go back to the streets, she thought. He needed a healthy diet, regular rest and exercise, checkups, heart medication. . . . As far as she knew, Social Services had not been able to come up with a solution. She made a mental note to check with the hospital social worker again.

Kyla glanced at her watch. Her time with Campy was almost up. Visits in CCU were limited to short ones for the patient's own good. Again, she wondered about

Ted. She wanted to ask Campy if he'd been by, but knew she couldn't. Besides, it was none of her business. Each day she avoided seeing Ted strengthened her resolve to forget him, forget their lovemaking.

Just then Kyla looked up to see Ted framed in the doorway. She couldn't remember him ever looking so sexy. Against her will, her eyes slid over him. He was dressed in a faded black sweatshirt with the sleeves pushed up to his elbows. How could she have forgotten how broad his chest was? How muscular his arms? And how well she fit into the curve of them? The jeans he wore low on his hips had the same comfortable quality of his sweatshirt and conformed to his body in places that brought the heat to her cheeks. The past few days she'd spent avoiding him had done nothing to dim the desire she felt for him.

She moistened her suddenly dry lips and met his eyes. What she read in his look made her even more uncomfortable. It was a look that said he remembered every curve of her body, and the texture and taste of it, even though she stood before him fully clothed.

Ted still had a devastating hold on her, she realized, but it was a hold she didn't have to allow. She pulled her gaze away.

Ted noticed her gaze shift. A frown wavered across her forehead like the electrocardiogram on Campy's monitor. What was it that was bothering her? Why did she withdraw from him? And why now? Just when he'd begun to daydream about sharing a home with her.

Perhaps not a domestic little cottage with a white picket fence. That wasn't his style. Or Kyla's. And certainly not an elaborate museum piece like the one he grew up in, but . . . A rambling old place in the country where their children could run free? An aging Victorian house with plenty of rooms and a wonderful old attic where kids could play on a rainy day? Mmm. That appealed to him. He and Kyla could make magical love every night under the gingerbread molding.

"It's about time," Campy snapped, startling Ted back to the present. "Did you find her?"

Kyla glanced over at Campy, then at Ted. What was Campy talking about? Who was Ted trying to find? Campy's face was lit with expectation. Ted was smiling.

"Yes, I found her. I found your daughter."

"Well, it took you long enough."

"You didn't give me a helluva lot to go on, you old buzzard. You were certainly expecting a miracle. Well, you got your miracle."

Campy gave an anticipatory look toward the doorway, then his face fell. "She's not coming."

"Did I say that? Did I say anything of the sort? She'll be in tonight. But next time you decide you're dying and want to renew old acquaintances, give me a little more to go on. I had all the guys at the paper working on it night and day. Last night we got a lead and . . . well, it paid off." Ted glanced over at Kyla. She was looking from one to the other, an expression of incredulity on her face.

"Louise," she said finally, remembering the woman's name listed as Next of Kin on Campy's ER form. It was the name he'd called Kyla once or twice that first night when he was so ill, obviously mistaking her for his daughter. Kyla smiled. So Campy's past was going to become part of the present.

"So, tell me about her. Is she all right?" Campy sat up, his roughened hands clutching the bed's side rail.

"She's fine and she's flying in from Virginia tonight, and that's all you're going to hear about it for now. If you don't calm down and get some sleep, you'll be in no shape to see her when she arrives," Ted said firmly.

"He's right," Kyla added. "I'll send the nurse in with something to help you rest."

Campy frowned at both of them, but leaned back against his pillow and nodded. "You'll be here, too?" he asked Kyla as she planted a kiss on his cheek before making her exit.

Kyla hesitated for a moment. It would mean seeing Ted again, something she didn't want to do. She looked down at the hopeful Campy and saw how important it was to him. "I'll be here," she said, fearing what her promise might cost her.

THE REUNION WAS A TEARFUL ONE and long overdue. Louise was a pretty woman, small and winsome with dark hair and Campy's blue eyes. Kyla liked her at once. She was married to an Air Force pilot and had two rambunctious sons—grandsons Campy had known nothing about. They were a powerful incentive for him to get well.

The old fellow clutched Louise's hand as if he were afraid she would disappear in a puff of smoke at any moment. Kyla longed to know what it had been that had torn the family apart so many years ago, but she couldn't ask. Whatever it had been, it hardly mattered anymore, she realized as she watched the two catch up on each other's lives. Whatever it had been that had caused her father to abandon her, Louise had obviously set aside the pain of it. She looked truly pleased to be reunited with him.

As soon as it was polite to do so, Kyla and Ted slipped off, leaving father and daughter talking a mile a minute.

"Finding Campy's daughter and bringing them together again was a pretty wonderful thing to do," Kyla said as they made their way toward the elevator.

"Yeah, well, what can I say? I'm a nice guy." Ted delivered a slow, sexy grin in her direction.

Kyla looked away. Yes, he was that and more. He was a very special guy. And she was in love with him—still. God help her!

"And now it's time for us." He ushered her into the waiting elevator and punched the button for the first floor. "Tonight, you and I are going to indulge our passions."

His words brought a host of sizzling images to Kyla's mind. Sweet, torturing images. Steamy, vivid images that heated the blood in her veins. But indulging her passions with this man was not something she could allow herself to do.

Ted could tell what she'd been thinking—if the hot color on her cheeks was any indication. He smiled down at her and trailed a lazy finger across the flaming blush. He wasn't going to allow her to pull away from him tonight. The evening beckoned, and he intended to spend it with her any way he could.

He could sense that Kyla wasn't ready to talk about what was bothering her. She seemed determined to hold herself just out of his reach, and for a while he would allow that. He'd keep their relationship light—if that's what it took—but he had to be with her. They had started something wonderful, something he wasn't about to forget. Something he wasn't about to let her forget.

When Kyla opened her mouth to offer some excuse, he silenced it with a kiss. A gentle kiss—he didn't want to frighten her—but a searing, sensuous kiss that reminded her of all that they had shared.

When the elevator lurched to a stop, Kyla came to her senses. "Ted, I . . . I can't go."

"Sure you can. Come on. It'll be fun. Just the two of us—and a whole crowd of people."

His green eyes danced with mischief, mischief Kyla had always found irresistible. A whole crowd of people? What was he up to?

"SPENCER! THIS IS A chocoholic's heaven!"

The aroma alone was driving her mad. She would gain ten pound merely smelling the stuff. Midnight-dark chocolate, white chocolate, chocolate with nuts. Fudge, kisses, mousses, tortes, each one a seductive treat that had her mouth watering.

He knew her weakness. Indulge their passions, indeed. Next to making love with Spencer, this sweet stuff ran a tight second!

"The Chocolate Lover's Festival. They hold it every year. Don't tell me you've never gone." Ted raised an eyebrow in surprise.

"No, never."

"Then you're in for a gastronomic adventure. I did a feature on the event last year for the paper and made a pig of myself sampling. What shall we try first?"

Kyla's eyes were as wide as a kid's in a candy store. She made a careful survey of the room, wondering if she could eat her way to the other side. Every chef in the city had brought his favorite taste temptations. Every candy store, bakery and restaurant was represented.

Finally, her gaze settled on a sultry six-layer Dutch chocolate confection. "I'll have that for a start."

"Make it two, Josef." Ted smiled at the tall-hatted chef rubbing his hands together in delight at Kyla's selection.

"*Monsieur* Spencer, *mon ami*, an extra big piece for you and your lady. Such a write-up you give me in your paper last year. Thanks to you, the customers—how you say?—come out my ears."

"*C'est magnifique*, Josef. But you have the customers because you create perfection."

The chef's round face lit up at Ted's words of praise and broke into a wreath of smiles as he watched Kyla enjoy each luxurious mouthful of torte.

Ted, too, enjoyed the sight. She ate with gusto, then plunged sticky fingers into her mouth to suck off the last little bit. It was a gesture so provocative he nearly came unglued. She had no idea the effect she had on him. He tore his eyes away from the distracting sight and tried to concentrate instead on finishing his own dessert.

"There's plenty more to sample," he said, leading Kyla to another booth.

They tried candies and mousse and truffles and admired the chocolate sculptures carved by some of the chefs. In the center of the room was a large vat of chocolate. For the grand finale of the evening, one of the city's TV news personalities would be dipped into it—all for charity, of course.

The TV cameras were assembling for the dunking. Ted spotted the reporter from the *Courier*, who was covering this year's event. He had Blood Hound in tow. Ted waved to them across the room, then absorbed himself in deciding which piece of fancy candy he wanted to try, tempting Kyla into sampling one as well.

"I can't eat another bite," she protested. She only hoped she wouldn't be sick in the morning from all the sugar she'd consumed already.

"You're a real powder puff, Kyla," he said and selected two dark bites which he popped into his mouth.

"And you are going to overdose on the stuff if you're not careful," she retorted.

"Mmm. What a way to go."

Kyla laughed.

Ted stopped to speak to one of the officials of the fete, introducing Kyla. Jack Springer was the owner of one of the large restaurants in Kansas City.

"Miss Bradford, with your permission I'd like to borrow your escort for a while," Jack said after greeting her warmly.

"Certainly." Kyla looked puzzled, but agreed to relinquish Ted for whatever purpose he had in mind.

"Spencer, we need someone to dunk into the vat. Wayne Wilson from Channel Seven didn't show and we're desperate."

Ted eyed the apparatus in the middle of the room as if it were a medieval torture chamber. "Oh, no, not me. Get yourself another boy," he protested vehemently.

"Come on, Spencer. People have pledged a lot of money to see someone take a bath in this stuff. You've got to do it."

"Channel Seven must have sent someone else to stand in for Wayne."

"Yeah, they sent a female. We'll look like real bad guys if we dunk a woman."

Ted sighed with resignation. He was trapped and he might as well give in gracefully. Jack Springer wasn't about to let him off the hook, and he couldn't let a woman take the plunge. He let Jack lead him away to change into something appropriate for a dip into warm chocolate. This should cure him of his craving for the stuff once and for all.

Kyla could hardly contain her amusement. She tried maintaining a sedate grin, but was soon laughing outright. She joined Blood Hound for a better view. She didn't want to miss this.

Soon Ted emerged wearing a pair of formfitting bicycling shorts and a tank top. Kyla's last laugh came out as a wheeze at the sight of his lithe body molded seductively into the bright blue spandex. The tight revealing shorts showed off his male endowments and she suddenly felt very warm under her light wool skirt and sweater. She was certain it had nothing to do with the temperature in the room.

Blood Hound edged in closer with his camera, his zoom lens at the ready. Ted was seated on the dunking stool, a half smile frozen on his face.

"Five, four, three," the announcer began the count-down. The crowd waited in anticipation. "Two, one, *splashdown.*"

Ted dropped into the vat. The crowd roared. Blood Hound managed to get several good shots before he broke into laughter.

Kyla laughed, too, but her chuckles subsided into a weak smile as Ted was lifted out of the swirling pool, his body sleek and dripping with chocolate. It was a sensuous sight she hadn't anticipated. He wiped the sticky mess away from his eyes, then ran his tongue slowly over his lips, lapping up the sweetness. His se-ductive grin invited her to sample the dark richness coating him. Their eyes held, and Kyla felt as if they were alone in the room.

"Tastes yummy," he said, when her breathing threatened to collapse.

He was teasing her, tempting her into a response. And she was responding, with a bone-melting weak-ness. She'd thought she could handle her emotions, thought she'd be safe from Ted's charms in a roomful of people. But she realized she wasn't safe anywhere within a thirty mile radius of the man.

She should run. Now. While there was still time. But Ted held her like a magnet. A part of her wished she'd never met him and another part of her wanted him to take her into his arms, chocolate and all.

One day, one day soon, she'd have to walk away. She knew that. The longer she waited, the more painful the parting would be. She knew that, too. But she'd have a few more memories to keep her warm in the years to come. Warm memories of Spencer and their brief time together.

"I DON'T KNOW ABOUT YOU, but I've had enough of this scene," Ted muttered when he rejoined her. All trace of chocolate was gone. He'd been treated to a long hot shower as a reward for his dunking. Now his skin glowed with a fresh-scrubbed look and his hair curled in damp tendrils over the tops of his ears. "How about working off all those calories we consumed. I know a congenial little establishment where we can dance."

She'd never danced with Ted before, but knew instinctively he'd be terrific. Could she trust herself in his arms? He smelled like soap and his green eyes smoldered with invitation. "Warm memories," she murmured.

"What?"

Kyla hadn't realized she'd spoken out loud. "Nothing. I . . . I just said it's warm in here."

"Then, let's go."

THEY WERE DANCING TOO SLOWLY to work off many calories, but Kyla wasn't complaining. The place was dimly lit, the dance floor small and intimate, the music mellow. Ted held her close, his arm encircling her waist, his lips brushing her cheek. A delicious warmth spread through her body, melting her limbs. It was a moment in time she wanted to capture so she could bring it out to savor at will.

Why had she let herself fall so deeply in love? When had it happened? And could she have stopped it?

Kyla sighed. Love had played a dirty trick on her. She and Ted had no future. Tonight was wonderful, but one day soon, she knew she'd have to pay the price for it.

The music ended. The couples separated and scattered to their respective tables. Ted's arm slid from her waist and Kyla stepped back, feeling suddenly alone and cold without his closeness.

To banish the feeling, she smiled brightly. She didn't intend to tuck tonight away into her mental memory box with any unpleasant thoughts. "You dance very well," she said as they made their way to their table at the edge of the dance floor.

"I should after all the money my mother spent on lessons. When I was five, she dressed me in a Little Lord Fauntleroy suit and sent me off to learn the social graces."

"That's why you smiled like a gentleman when they dunked you into the chocolate tonight!"

"And if you had any manners, Kyla Bradford, you wouldn't have been laughing with such abandon."

Kyla looked away self-consciously. She was glad he'd noticed her laughter instead of her admiration of his body in chocolate spandex. It was another memory she didn't intend to give up.

They danced a few more dances before calling it quits and making their way out into the night. The wind whipped from the north with a blast of arctic cold. The sky was clear and the stars shone brightly, seeming closer than usual.

"Race you to the car," Ted challenged.

Kyla laughed and did her best to beat him. "No fair. You have longer legs," she cried in defense as she lost by two yards.

"Next time I'll give you a head start," he said, brushing an errant curl away from her face.

Her breath glistened in the crisp night air, then mingled with his as he leaned close and met her lips with his. They were as sweet and warm as a peach in the spring sunshine and every bit as lush. He nipped and savored the taste of them, before dipping his tongue inside to take all that she offered. But he knew it wasn't enough. He wanted all of her. Not only tonight, but forever.

Then she was in his arms. He could feel the pounding of her heart even though they were bundled into winter coats. His own heart thundered as loudly. He bent his head for another taste of her, but the sound of a car squealing to a stop beside them interrupted the moment.

Ted and Kyla wheeled around to see two policemen smiling at them through the window of a patrol car.

"Ain't love sweet, Andy," one of them said, rolling down the window.

"Sure is, Sam," the other one answered with a chuckle. "You two want to move along?"

Kyla tried to look properly chastised, but she was choking back a smile.

"Sure thing, officers." Ted gave them a little salute, then dragged Kyla off to the car before that smile turned into out-and-out laughter.

Safely inside the car, the dam broke. Kyla's laughter spilled over.

"That wasn't funny," Ted pretended to chide. But Kyla's hilarity was infectious. One look at her lack of composure and he was caught up in it. Soon he was laughing so hard he had to wipe away the tears.

Once he could see to drive, he aimed the car in the direction of Kyla's apartment. They had had a fun time tonight. He'd promised himself he'd keep their relationship light, and he wouldn't spoil it now by making demands on her she wasn't ready for. But did she have to tempt him with that wide sexy smile of hers?

"I'm glad I went this evening," Kyla said as they climbed the stairs to the carriage house.

She sighed as she thought of the memories she had to store away. It would be so easy to slip into Ted's arms again, to finish the kiss the policemen had interrupted. In the warm fuzzy mood she was in, it would be so easy to make love with Ted once more. But could her memory bank deal with that in the years to come?

She didn't think so.

"Brrr! Kyla, it's freezing in here?" Ted stepped into the apartment. "Where's your thermostat?"

"Over there. On the wall."

Ted examined it. The dial was set on seventy-two, but it registered fifty-four. "Where's your furnace?"

"Downstairs. In the storage room off the garage." Kyla pulled her coat tighter around her. What was wrong? It had been nice and toasty when she'd left. She paced the living room until Ted returned.

"The furnace is out. I tried to relight it, but no luck." There was a smudge of dust on his chin. Kyla reached up to wipe it away, but he caught her hand and kissed her palm. She felt instantly warmer. "You can't stay here tonight," he said.

"Don't be silly. I'll be fine. I'll put a log on the fireplace and dig out my sleeping bag. I'll be as snug as a bug in a rug."

"And what happens when the fire dies out in the middle of the night?"

"I'll put on another log."

"You're going home with me. I'll give you three minutes to pack a bag, and if you haven't done it by then, I'm doing it for you."

TED'S APARTMENT WAS a third-floor disaster. As he hurried around picking up his scattered belongings, Kyla poked about, hiding a smile at the way he kept house. "Ted, I can't believe you live this way."

"It's not dirty," he said defensively. "Just...cluttered. I suppose it's a sort of rebellion against the way I was raised. Pretty silly, huh?" He came up behind her with an armload of clean socks and planted a kiss on her neck.

Kyla tried to ignore the sudden heat spreading through her. "Are these your parents?" She picked up a leather-framed photograph from the bookshelf, admiring the picture of the dignified couple.

"Yes," he answered, dumping the socks and taking the picture from her. "I haven't seen my father for years. Watching Louise with Campy tonight reminded me I have some fence-mending of my own to do."

He set the picture back in its dusty spot on the bookshelf and led Kyla toward the sofa. "I never approved of my father's money or the ruthless way he acquired it. I suppose that's why I came down so hard on Leonard Daniels. I saw a lot of my father in him."

"So, are you going to lighten up on Leonard in your articles?"

"No. Not if the man deserves what I write." He saw the surprise in her eyes. "I'm a reporter, Kyla. A good one. I do the job I have to."

"I know that, Ted."

Her voice was a whisper, but it rang with the beginnings of trust, a belief in him that made him feel proud. He only wished she trusted him in other ways, as well.

For the first time that evening, silence stretched before them. Ted spoke to fill the awkward gap. "The bed's made up. I'll sleep out here if you like." He touched her hair, letting its silkiness slide through his fingers. "I know something's bothering you, Kyla, but I don't know what it is. I wish you'd talk about it. Whatever it is, we can work it out."

Kyla bit her lower lip and fought to hold back the tears swimming just below the surface. Ted was wonderful. There'd never be another man more perfect for her—or more wrong. She would always love him. She'd never forget his laughing eyes, his crazy smile, the timbre of his voice when he spoke her name. She'd always remember the touch of his fingertips on her breast, the sweet madness she felt when they made love.

She threw her arms around his neck and kissed him. "You're a good man, Ted Spencer."

"Only good?"

A smile hovered at the edges of her mouth. "Maybe . . . spectacular."

"That's more like it." He trailed a finger across her bottom lip. He could sense the sadness in her. It had been there all evening. She'd hidden it behind her smiles, her banter, but he'd seen it. Some sixth sense told him it had to do with their relationship. And that same sixth sense told him it was big enough to destroy everything between them. If she didn't talk about it, he was certain that it would. "Talk to me, love. Tell me what's making you sad."

"I'm not sad, Spencer," she said, concentrating on the frayed point of his shirt collar. She couldn't bear seeing the questions haunting his beautiful green eyes.

He wanted answers, but how could she tell him? She didn't even know how far he intended their relationship to go. He'd never mentioned love, much less marriage. At least, not marriage to her. All she knew was that she loved him. And if she had any sense at all, she'd walk away from him tonight and never look back.

Ted lifted her chin, studying her face. She saw his troubled smile and knew she hadn't fooled him with her quick reply.

With no heat in her apartment, she couldn't even go home. Damn her luck! She could go to Allie's. Or Leah's. Or even a hotel. She could drag out her sleeping bag like she'd threatened. But she knew Ted would never let her sleep in the cold.

She clenched her fists in frustration. Was this how Campy felt the night Ted dragged him into the ER? Ted had been doing what was best for Campy. But was he doing what was best for her? When just one look at him made her want him so much her insides ached.

All he had to do was kiss her and she'd be lost. She had to go, she had to get out of here before . . .

Ted stroked her cheek, then leaned toward her, kissing each eyelid in turn. She was screaming on the inside. She couldn't let him . . .

Then his mouth found hers, brushing it so lightly she felt her breath snatched from her. She was drowning in the soft sensation of his lips, the nip of his teeth, the flick of his tongue. She was his prisoner as surely as if she were bound hand and foot.

Her body pulsed with raw need, her veins flowed with liquid fire. All conscious thought fled from her. She was capable only of responding to his gentle assault.

"Let me love you tonight," Ted whispered, his voice taut with restraint. "Let me show you how very much you mean to me."

She nodded her assent; she had no power to do otherwise.

With caressing hands, he stripped her of her clothing. She shivered slightly as the cool air of the room brushed her heated skin. But it did nothing to cool the passion building to a fever pitch within her.

Ted's clothes followed hers, forgotten where they fell. He reached over the arm of the sofa and flicked off the lamp, leaving only the night's soft moonlight melting over them. Scattering large pillows onto the floor in front of the bay window, he created a cozy setting for their lovemaking. The room was silent except for the solid-sounding tick of an old mantel clock and the deafening beat of her heart, as Ted invited her down onto the pillowed floor.

"You've been out of my arms too long," he murmured. "I missed you."

"And I missed you," she answered, admiring his lean taut body beside her.

Her eager eyes couldn't get enough of him. She caressed his abdomen where the moonlight streaked across it. He trembled as her fingers moved lower, touching, stroking, then a groan of pleasure tore from his throat as her hand closed over him.

"Ah, Kyla, you little wench," he gasped, and gave her a seductive dose of her own medicine as he found a few sensitive areas on her body.

Kyla shuddered with delight as he tortured her with soft kisses, caressing her to near-madness with his tongue. The responsive places his mouth didn't find, his fingers did, dancing over her fiery flesh, driving her to the point of no return.

She arched toward him, needing more, demanding more, until he gave her all of himself. With their bodies united as one, they moved in a primal rhythm. She breathed his name, he whispered hers. It felt as if they'd always belonged to each other and always would. Together they were transported beyond the moment, climbing, soaring, higher and higher, beyond the mood. And then their excitement exploded into a million shimmering moonbeams that fell to earth with them.

Breathless, tangled in each other's arms, Ted nuzzled her neck. "I was too busy showing you how much I love you to say the words, so I'll say them now. I love you, Kyla Bradford."

Kyla was silent for a long moment, then her arms encircled his neck. "And I love you," she whispered softly.

Ted heard the words. They were the ones he'd longed to hear her say. But he also heard the tears in her voice and a shiver ran up his spine.

10

THEY SPENT EACH DAY of the next two weeks stealing as much time as they could from their busy schedules. Kyla tried not to think of the future, but lived for the moment, silencing her thoughts when they intruded on the present.

She and Ted laughed and made love; they watched old movies, kissing in the darkened balcony like two starry-eyed teenagers; they visited the museum, an art exhibit; they dined elegantly, then went to a Go-Kart race still dressed in their evening finery. Life was perfect.

Kyla didn't think about the fact that it was an artificial perfection, a temporary happiness. To her it was a beautiful interlude, a time in her life that would never come again.

On nights Kyla worked, Ted often shared supper breaks with her in the cafeteria, carrying in barbecue or Chinese food to avoid the horrid hospital fare. Tonight, he'd had mushroom pizza delivered.

Louise joined the two of them at their usual table, half-hidden behind a jungle of green plastic plants. Although pleased with her father's recovery, she was upset that he refused to come and live with her. Campy insisted he had no intention of changing his living quarters, heart attack or no heart attack. He wasn't about to give up his freedom for his daughter's confining house, even if it did have nine rooms and sat on three acres of land.

"How can I go back to Virginia and leave him to roam the streets. I'd worry myself sick every day," she said, twisting her napkin into a useless shred of paper. Her untouched slice of pizza sat in front of her. "Now that I've found him, I can't lose him again."

Ted slid his hand over hers. "Louise, don't worry. I promise you, you won't be going home alone. My little plan will work. Just have your sons here tomorrow afternoon and leave the rest to me." He looked over at Kyla and winked.

Kyla smiled back. She hoped Ted was right. Louise loved her father in spite of the fact that he'd walked out of her life when she was a child. The past could not be rewoven, but the two of them could share a happier future—if only Campy wouldn't be so stubborn.

Louise sighed. "The boys are so excited to be coming to Kansas City to see their grandfather, but I'm just not sure—"

"I know Campy," Ted interrupted. "He's a sucker for little kids. They'll tame him like a pussycat in no time. Trust me."

The frown on her forehead eased a little. "You've done so much already, Ted."

KYLA WANTED TO SEE Campy's face when he met his grandsons for the first time. She was working the day shift and decided to slip away from the ER long enough to sneak up to the solarium on the third floor where the meeting was to take place. The boys could not go to their grandfather's room—hospital rules—but a nurse would wheel Campy to the sunroom. Kyla didn't want to intrude on the family's time together; she wanted to give them a chance to get acquainted, so she'd keep out of sight and watch from a distance. Halfway up the little-used staircase, however, she met with trouble.

"Miss Bradford, aren't you a tad off your beaten path? What are you doing up here?"

How was she to know Wallace would be trekking up the stairs? Was he turning into a fitness freak at his age? "Just taking a short-cut," she answered.

"A short-cut to where?" he asked pointedly.

"To, uh, a staff meeting."

"A staff meeting?"

"A boring one on . . . on Keeping Health Care Costs Low in the Emergency Setting," she improvised quickly.

He drew his thick brows together. "I wonder why I didn't hear about this meeting?"

"Don't know, Wallace. Gotta run. I don't want to be late." She continued up the stairs, leaving him scratching his head in bewilderment. The topic of hospital finances was near and dear to the man's heart. He'd spend the rest of the afternoon trying to find out where the meeting was and why he hadn't been invited to attend.

As she neared the solarium she saw that Campy had not yet arrived. Louise was there—and her two sons. Kyla knew their ages were four and six. Louise had talked endlessly about them. Although their mother had them scrubbed and polished and dressed in their best clothes for the occasion, they looked as if they'd rather be scouting frogs in a muddy stream.

Right now, Ted held them spellbound with some sleight of hand he was demonstrating. Kyla could hear the boys' wild squeals of delight, which they struggled to control. Their dark heads were bent over the card trick, watching intently, hoping their eyes were quicker than Ted's hands.

But it was Ted's face that held Kyla's attention—the happiness his expression reflected. He was a natural for fatherhood; it fit him like a second skin. Her heart did a painful somersault in her chest as the obvious was hammered home. Ted had a lot of love to give. He needed children of his own.

She turned to run from the overpowering scene, wanting to hide from the reality of it, but instead collided with Campy and his wheelchair. The old fellow let loose with a loud curse that shocked his nurse and, no doubt, his daughter. Kyla mumbled her apologies, avoiding Campy's piercing scrutiny and hurried down the hall.

"What in thunder's gotten into that woman," Campy said, his eyes following her quick retreat.

Ted had looked up at the sound of the commotion. He'd caught only a brief glimpse of Kyla's face, but it had been enough for him to witness the pain ravaging it. His forehead wrinkled in a puzzled frown. The past two weeks had been so wonderful. He'd hoped whatever was bothering Kyla had been laid to rest. Now, he knew it hadn't been. But what was it that was bothering her? Why had she run away from this harmless little family scene?

Whatever it was, he intended to find out.

Louise seemed to have everything under control in the solarium. No introductions were necessary. Campy and his grandsons had sized up one another quickly and were fast becoming friends. Ted would have liked to stay and watch the boys sand the rough edges off their grandfather, but the pain he'd glimpsed in Kyla's face had been all too real.

"It doesn't look like you need me any longer," he whispered to Louise and hurried off down the corridor.

He reached the ER only to discover that Kyla had already been there, snatched up her coat and left two minutes before he'd arrived—and five minutes before her shift ended. He knew she was not in the habit of leaving work early; something had shaken her badly.

He set his jaw in determination. This time she was not going to hide behind evasions. He intended to get to the bottom of this, even if he had to shake the answers out of her.

When he reached the parking lot, he caught her battered blue Mustang disappearing through the far exit. His own car sat five rows away.

By the time he exited the lot and eased into the afternoon freeway traffic, Kyla was long gone. Cursing the slow moving tractor-trailer rig in front of him, he laid on the horn, but the driver of the lumbering behemoth was apparently unimpressed by the noise.

When he could finally change lanes, he did so with a wild squeal of tires. His only hope was to catch up to Kyla at the carriage house. But once he reached her apartment, there was no sign of her or that she'd been there. The driveway was empty, the mail overflowing its box. In discouragement he slumped down in his seat, staring morosely at her front door.

He didn't know where she might have gone or how he might go about finding her. All he knew was that she was hurting and he didn't even know why. Dejected, he wheeled his car around and pulled out of her driveway. He didn't know what direction to go. It didn't matter; he wouldn't be able to find her.

After ten minutes of aimless driving, he found himself at the park nearby. He decided to walk for a while, then drive by her place again; it was all he could do.

He pulled his collar up against the biting north wind and jammed his hands into his pockets. He knew the ducks wouldn't be there at this time of the year—it was too cold—but he headed in that direction anyway.

Then, he saw her.

She sat, huddled on the bench in front of the pond, seemingly impervious to the weather. He wanted to take her in his arms, hold her, protect her from whatever demons had made her run away today. He approached her softly as one might an easily frightened fawn.

"Kyla," he whispered her name.

Startled, she jumped up from the bench, her eyes immediately wary. They were red-rimmed from crying, but she still looked beautiful to him. He tipped the collar of her coat up around her neck to ward off the chilly breeze and took her bare hands into his to warm them.

"You shouldn't be out here without a hat or gloves. It's cold, in case you haven't noticed," he chided her.

Kyla lowered her head. She hadn't noticed the cold. She hadn't noticed much of anything since she'd seen Ted playing so comfortably with Louise's sons. "I'll be all right. Don't worry about me."

"That's what people do when they love each other. They worry. A lot."

She pulled away. She didn't want to hear him say these things—not anymore. It hurt too much. "Well, don't."

"Don't worry? Or don't love you?"

"Don't do either," she choked out the words as if they were being torn from her insides.

Ted brushed her cheek with his knuckles. "I'm afraid it's too late for that. I love you very much, Kyla. I don't know what's wrong, but whatever it is we'll work it out,

I promise you. Just talk to me. Tell me why you ran away today."

She reached a hand up and touched his face, then withdrew it as if she'd been burned. "There . . . there's something about me you don't know. I shouldn't have let myself love you. Not once I knew."

"Not once you knew what?" He captured her hand, determined not to let her pull away.

"About your childhood."

"My childhood. What does my childhood have to do with this, with us? Kyla, you're not making sense."

She drew a ragged breath. "Ted, we don't belong together."

"That's where you're wrong, Kyla dear. We very much belong together. For now and forever. I want to marry you."

Kyla's shaky breath caught in her throat. It was what she wanted, too. But it couldn't work. "That's not all you want. You also want children."

His arms encircled her waist. "I thought it might be a nice touch."

She put her hands on his arms and pushed hard, breaking his hold. "That's the problem. Ted, don't you see. You had a lonely childhood and you want to erase that loneliness by having a big wonderful family. And you should have that family. I saw you with Campy's grandkids today. You'll make a terrific father. If anyone is a natural for parenthood, it's you."

"And you'd make a terrific mother. So, what's the problem?"

Kyla sighed and took a few steps away from him. This was the hard part. She didn't want to see the love die on his face when she told him. She couldn't bear that.

"Ted, I had arthritis when I was a student nurse. I barely made it through training and nursing was something I wanted very badly. The disease... incapacitated me for many months at a time—"

"Arthritis?" He whirled her around to face him. "But you're fine—"

"Now. Yes, now I'm fine. I was lucky I wasn't left with deformities."

"My God, Kyla." He grabbed her and held her, rocking her like a child. "I had no idea what you'd been through."

Being in his arms felt so good. She wanted to hide there forever, safe and warm in his embrace. He smelled like fresh air and leather. She realized she couldn't stay in his arms, no matter how much she wanted to. She broke free of him and sat down on the bench.

"There's more," she said.

Ted dropped down beside her. She wished he wouldn't sit so close. Telling him the rest would be difficult enough.

"The doctors said the disease could recur at stressful times in my life, such as... during pregnancy. Ted, I can't give you the big family you want. I can't give you children."

He stared at her in stony silence. It was what she'd feared—the love dying on his face, in his eyes, in his heart. She had to get away. "I'm sorry," she whispered so quietly it could have been mistaken for the sound of the breeze.

Then she ran. She ran until she thought her lungs would burst. She'd go where she always went when she needed to heal. Home. Back to the rolling hills covered with apple trees. It didn't matter that it was winter and the trees were bare. She had two days off. Not that she could heal in two days. She couldn't heal in two years. But she could gather strength, the strength she needed to forget.

TED SAT ON THE HARD PARK BENCH, staring vacantly at the riffles the wind stirred on the pond's glassy surface. The temperature had dropped a few chilling degrees as the afternoon edged toward sunset. His nose was red and his feet had begun to lose all feeling.

Kyla's revelation had stunned him. He should have pulled her into his arms, kissed her, told her none of it mattered. But, he hadn't, and now she was gone.

He stood up to stretch his legs. Sharp needles of pain stabbed his lower limbs as his circulation returned. He had to walk. He had to think.

He'd always expected to have children one day, lots of them, their laughter filling every corner of his house and his life. Kyla was right. He wanted to blot out the loneliness of his childhood. He didn't want a silent empty house like the one he'd grown up in.

Climbing the slight rise overlooking the pond, he sat down heavily on the winter-dried grass. This was where he'd kissed Kyla the first time, he remembered with a sudden wrenching in his gut. Even then he'd realized she was special to him, that he wanted her in his life. His mind hadn't worked out the details as yet, but his heart had known.

He picked up a handful of leaves and threw them, watching them flutter to the ground. Dead, lifeless, like he felt on the inside. It was Kyla who gave him life. She was filled with it.

Slowly, leadenly, he got to his feet and started back across the park toward his car.

"THEY'RE SPRINGIN' ME from this place tomorrow," Campy told Ted two days later. "Them nurses will have to find somebody else to inflict their pain and suffering on."

"I heard they've planned a celebration for the minute they wheel you out the door."

"Harrumph!"

"I also heard you're going home with Louise," Ted added more seriously.

Campy tossed down his spoon. He'd been eating a bowl of peaches, his afternoon snack. Beside it was a plate of oatmeal cookies, a container of ice cream and an orange. The man had done nothing but eat since he'd come through the hospital doors.

"That woman been talkin' again?"

"No, your grandsons told me."

"Well, they ain't got the story right. I'm goin' for a visit, nothin' else. And those two know it. I ain't made them no promises."

Ted groaned to himself as Campy exchanged the dish of peaches for the ice cream. Unless he'd missed his guess, that visit would soon become a permanent stay. And he'd better warn Louise to lay in a hefty supply of groceries.

"Where is Louise, anyway?" Ted asked.

Campy coughed and sputtered a bit before answering. "Out buyin' me some new duds to wear. Says I have to look 'presentable.' That woman's gonna turn my life inside out. I can feel it in my bones." He polished off the ice cream and started in on the plate of cookies. "I was hopin' Kyla'd be by before I left," he continued between bites. "I ain't seen her in two days. Same length of time you been mopin' around. You gonna tell me what's wrong?"

Ted's eyebrows knitted into a vee. "Who says I've been moping?"

"I didn't just fall down with the last rain. Old Campy knows a few things. And you been mopin'."

It didn't take someone with second sight to realize that, Ted supposed. The truth was he'd been miserable without Kyla. He'd tried to find her, but she hadn't been home. The only information he could get out of her friends in the ER was that she had a few days off.

"You gonna marry that girl?"

Ted looked over at his friend's earnest face. Campy cared a great deal for Kyla. His life, whether he admitted it or not, was suddenly full of promise, and he wanted the same for Kyla and Ted. Ted knew that. "Everything's not that simple," he answered.

"Simple? You gotta have simple? I thought all you needed was love. Don't you love her?"

"Yes, I love her." He had no doubts about that. The past two sleepless nights had reminded him how much he needed her in his life and in his bed.

"Does she love you?"

Kyla had told him she did in a hundred different ways. And it was a love he didn't want to lose. "Yes," he answered.

Campy gave a triumphant smile. "Sounds simple to me."

Maybe it could be that simple, after all. Ted paced the floor of the small hospital room. Perhaps he was some kind of fool to think that a little bit of noise and laughter could silence the past. He couldn't erase those years any more than Campy could wipe away his. And Campy wasn't trying to. He was going forward, not looking back. "Maybe you're right, McDuff."

He decided to try his new reasoning out on his friend. Campy already knew about Ted's childhood. And he knew Ted loved kids—that fact had become abundantly clear when he was around Campy's grandsons. What Campy didn't know was that Kyla could not risk pregnancy to give Ted the family he wanted,

Campy let out a low whistle when Ted told him. "If I know Kyla, this is tearin' that girl apart," he theorized.

Ted was certain it was. "I've got to find her, McDuff. I've got to tell her I love her. Our love's the important thing. Nothing else matters."

"Yep. And you better get it all straightened out before I leave. I wanna know everything's all right between you two before I get on that plane," Campy said.

Ted wasn't sure that was possible—Campy left tomorrow—but he was sure as hell going to try.

KYLA HAD SPENT THE FIRST DAY of her retreat wandering the orchard's hills and feeling sorry for herself. Her parents had realized something serious was on their daughter's mind and left her alone. Kyla had been grateful for the privacy.

She'd gone home to forget about Ted and everything he meant to her. But how could she forget the tingle of her skin when he touched her, the hush in his voice when he whispered he loved her? She couldn't. Everything about him was etched into her memory, branded into her heart.

Instead of trying to forget him, she began to examine her fears. She'd always kept abreast of the latest in medical news, particularly when it related to her type of arthritis. She knew that with the advances being made in obstetrics, she could be monitored throughout a pregnancy without too much risk. What she didn't know was whether she had enough courage to take that risk.

The soul-searching was painful. The memory of her illness was still fresh in her mind, her accompanying fears very real. But overriding it all was Ted and his love. Could she possibly live without it, without him?

When she finally came to grips with her cowardice, she was ready to return to the city. She made an appointment with her doctor to discuss her options. Now, as she stepped out of his waiting room into the corridor, she knew she'd made the right decision.

KYLA HAD TRIED ALL EVENING to find a quiet moment to call Ted and tell him she needed to talk to him. But the ER had stayed busy. Three lacerations, a nosebleed, a fractured wrist, an asthma attack, a dog bite, two car accidents. And Wallace.

The administrator wanted to discuss staffing in her department. Could she possibly get by with one less nurse on each shift? he'd asked. After the parade of patients they'd just had, Wallace could count himself lucky Kyla hadn't inflicted such bodily harm on him that he needed the ER's services himself.

He'd finally left, suggesting they discuss it at a later time. Fortunately, he'd missed her parting comment: *When pigs fly, Wallace!*

Kyla had just reached for the phone and begun dialing Ted's number when the double glass doors of Emergency opened again. Her sense of déjà vu was overwhelming. Jane, the admitting clerk, supported Ted Spencer against her tiny frame. This time he was limping. She smiled to herself as he seemed to be trying to make up his mind which one of his extremities was injured. What was he up to?

"Put him in Room One," she told Jane and suppressed a chuckle.

As she had that very first night that Ted had come into her life, she couldn't help admiring his body. Only now she knew that body in an intimate way.

"Thank you, Jane. I'll take over," she said, dismissing the woman, all the while her eyes communicating with Ted's.

Why had he come? It wasn't because of an injured ankle. Of that she was certain. She tried to read the answer in his face, but his expression remained inscrutable. The door closed with a firm click behind her, startling her. She'd wanted to tell him about her decision, but now that they were alone she was suddenly dumbstruck.

His warm brown curls looked windtossed. Or had he been dragging his fingers through his hair in indecision over coming here tonight?

"I had to see you," he said, jamming his hands deep into his pockets.

"About a sore ankle?"

He looked down, studying the tips of his well-worn sneakers. Then his head raised, a grin spread across the generous curves of his mouth. "I knew it was a dumb idea. You wouldn't fall for it a second time."

"A second time! I didn't fall for it the first time, if you remember."

"I remember. I remember a lot of things," he said, looking suddenly wistful. "Kyla, I came here to tell you that I love you and I still want to marry you. Our love is the important thing, not whether or not we have children. I want you in my life any way I can have you. Nothing else matters."

Kyla felt warm all over. It was nice to know he wanted her, but she knew it might not be enough for him one day. "It could matter, Ted. You mean what you say now, but one day it could come between us."

"Kyla, I will always hear the silence of my childhood. I was foolish to think a house full of kids could change the past—"

She took a few steps toward him and put her fingers to his lips. "We could try." Smiling, she went on. "Today I went to see my doctor. I had to know if I could safely have a child."

He took her fingers in his hands and kissed the tips of them. "Kyla, that wasn't necessary—"

"He said that with special care I could do it."

"You love me that much?"

She nodded.

"Well, I love you too much to let you take that risk."

Kyla didn't want to argue with him. She wanted to marry him. "Is this the way our marriage is going to be?" she asked, giving him one of her wily smiles. "One big disagreement?"

He cradled her face in his hands. "Probably. But I think we can find time to make love, too."

She looked up at him. "And have children?"

"We'll have to spend some time arguing about that, Kyla, there are kids out there who need a home—should we decide to fill up all the corners of one some-day."

Her face lit up. "Ted, that's a wonderful idea. We could do both."

Ted laughed. "What makes me think I'm going to lose every argument we ever have." He swept her into his arms and lowered his head to kiss her.

It was a gentle kiss at first, a kiss full of promise and commitment. Then, it deepened into passion, the passion they'd never been able to deny. They were oblivious to the rest of the world outside the door, as they tested and savored, knowing they could never get enough of each other.

"Can you get out of here early?" Ted asked, his voice choked with desire.

A smile wove at the edges of Kyla's mouth. "Wallace did suggest earlier that we get by with one less nurse…"

"And?"

"I argued with him."

"Silly girl."

HARLEQUIN *Temptation*

COMING NEXT MONTH

#309 AFTER HOURS Gina Wilkins

Executive assistant Angelique St. Clair knew the office gossips said she and her boss, Rhys Wakefield, were made for each other; they were both cold, intimidating workaholics. And maybe they were—during business hours. But after hours, the heat they generated was enough to melt a polar ice cap... and the heart of one very cool CEO!

#310 TALISMAN Laurien Berenson

Woodbury, Connecticut, wasn't New York City. And Kelly Ransome wasn't a city woman. She was straightforward and freshly scrubbed... and came equipped with three Dobermans! But that didn't stop journalist Eric Devane from pursuing her. After all, Eric had an overexuberant Rotweiller pup on his hands, and Kelly was a dog trainer— the best. And Eric Devane *only* pursued the best.

#311 HIDDEN MESSAGES Regan Forest

Vacationing on a Scottish isle, Laurie MacDonald fell in love with Eric Sinclair—part Gypsy, part rogue and all sex appeal. But then she discovered his love was a deception and she plotted a fitting revenge... only she couldn't convince her heart she was better off without him.

#312 ALWAYS Jo Morrison

Tanner McNeil wanted a wife. After eight years of trying to convince footloose Jodi to settle down with him on the farm, he'd given up. Meeting Lara Jamison restored his hope in happy endings. But Lara suspected that perfect as they were for each other in bed, Tanner was still seeing Jodi in his dreams....

THE LOVES OF A CENTURY

Join American Romance in a nostalgic look back at the twentieth century—at the lives and loves of American men and women from the turn-of-the-century to the dawn of the year 2000.

Journey through the decades from the dance halls of the 1900s to the discos of the seventies... from Glenn Miller to the Beatles... from Valentino to Newman... from corset to miniskirt... from beau to significant other.

Relive the moments... recapture the memories.

Watch for all the CENTURY OF AMERICAN ROMANCE titles in Harlequin American Romance. In one of the four American Romance books appearing each month, for the next ten months, we'll take you back to a decade of the twentieth century, where you'll relive the years and rekindle the romance of days gone by.

Don't miss a day of A CENTURY OF AMERICAN ROMANCE.

The women... the men... the passions... the memories...

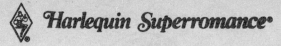

Harlequin Superromance

Hamilton
H·O·U·S·E

A powerful restaurant conglomerate that draws the best and brightest to its executive ranks. Now almost eighty years old, Vanessa Hamilton, the founder of Hamilton House, must choose a successor.
Who will it be?

Matt Logan: He's always been the company man, the quintessential team player. But tragedy in his daughter's life and a passionate love affair made him make some hard choices....

Paula Steele: Thoroughly accomplished, with a sharp mind, perfect breeding and looks to die for, Paula thrives on challenges and wants to have it all ... but is this right for her?

Grady O'Connor: Working for Hamilton House was his salvation after Vietnam. The war had messed him up but good and had killed his storybook marriage. He's been given a second chance—only he doesn't know what the hell he's supposed to do with it....

Harlequin Superromance invites you to enjoy Barbara Kaye's dramatic and emotionally resonant miniseries about mature men and women making life-changing decisions. Don't miss:

- CHOICE OF A LIFETIME—a July 1990 release.
  - CHALLENGE OF A LIFETIME
    —a December 1990 release.
- CHANCE OF A LIFETIME—an April 1991 release.